THE COURAGEOUS CAPTAIN AMERICA™

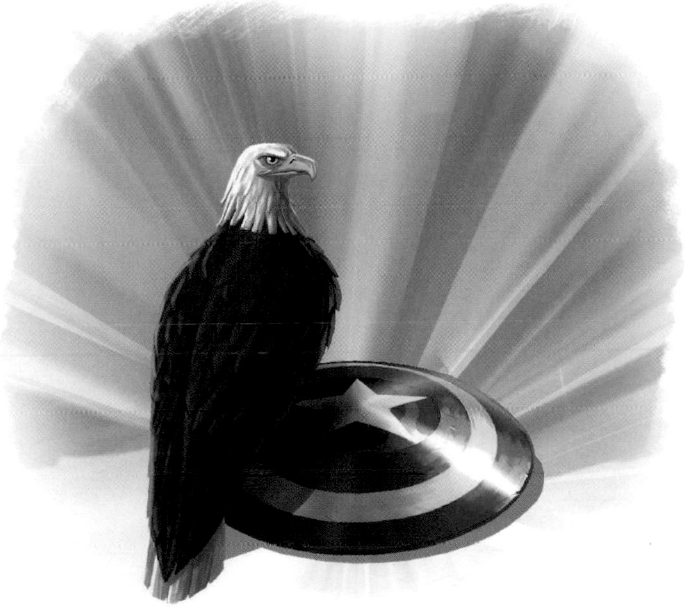

AN ORIGIN STORY

Based on the Marvel comic book series **Captain America**
Adapted by Rich Thomas
Illustrated by Val Semeiks, Bob McLeod,
Hi-Fi Colour and Design, and The Storybook Art Group

MARVEL
New York

For Duke
—RT

MARVEL

Printed in the United States of America
First Edition
13579108642
G942-9090-6-11152
ISBN 978-1-4231-4464-9

SUSTAINABLE FORESTRY INITIATIVE
Certified Fiber Sourcing
www.sfiprogram.org

SGS-SFICOC-0130
FOR TEXT ONLY

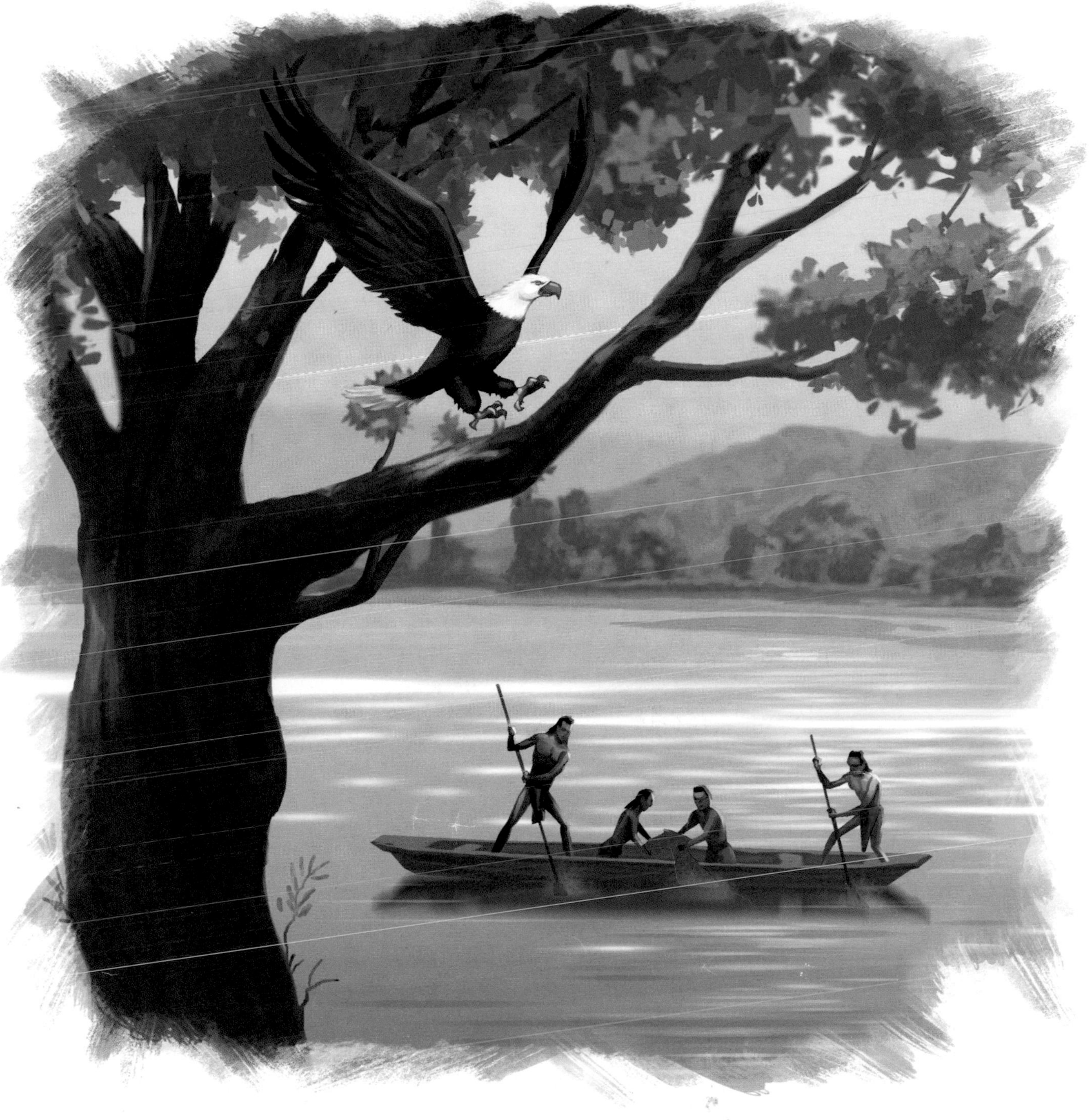

Before you were born—in fact, long before even the oldest person you know had been born—a peaceful little island sat right off the mainland of a place that was called different things by all the different nations of people who lived there.

As time went on,

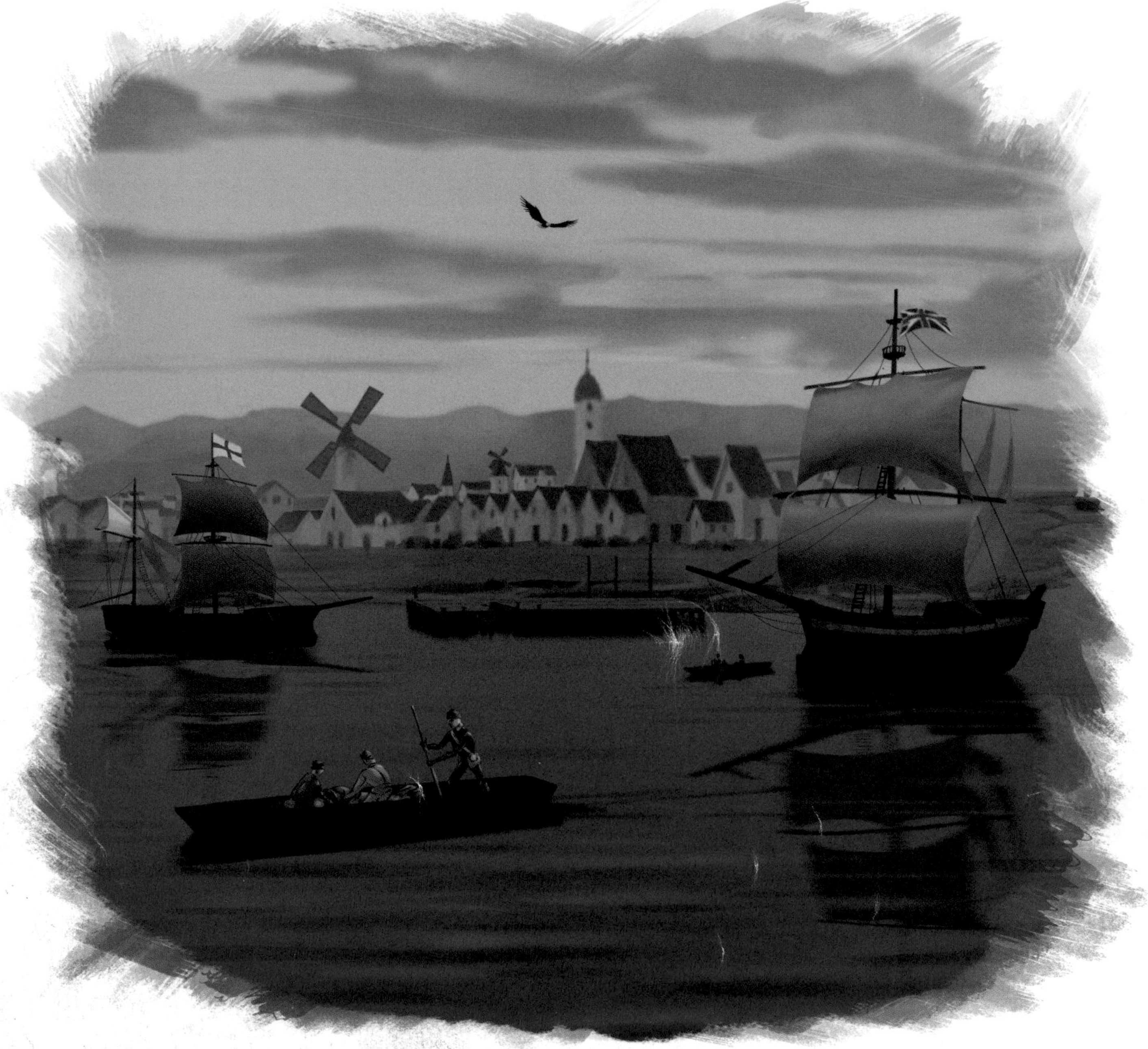

more and more people came
to this **little island.**

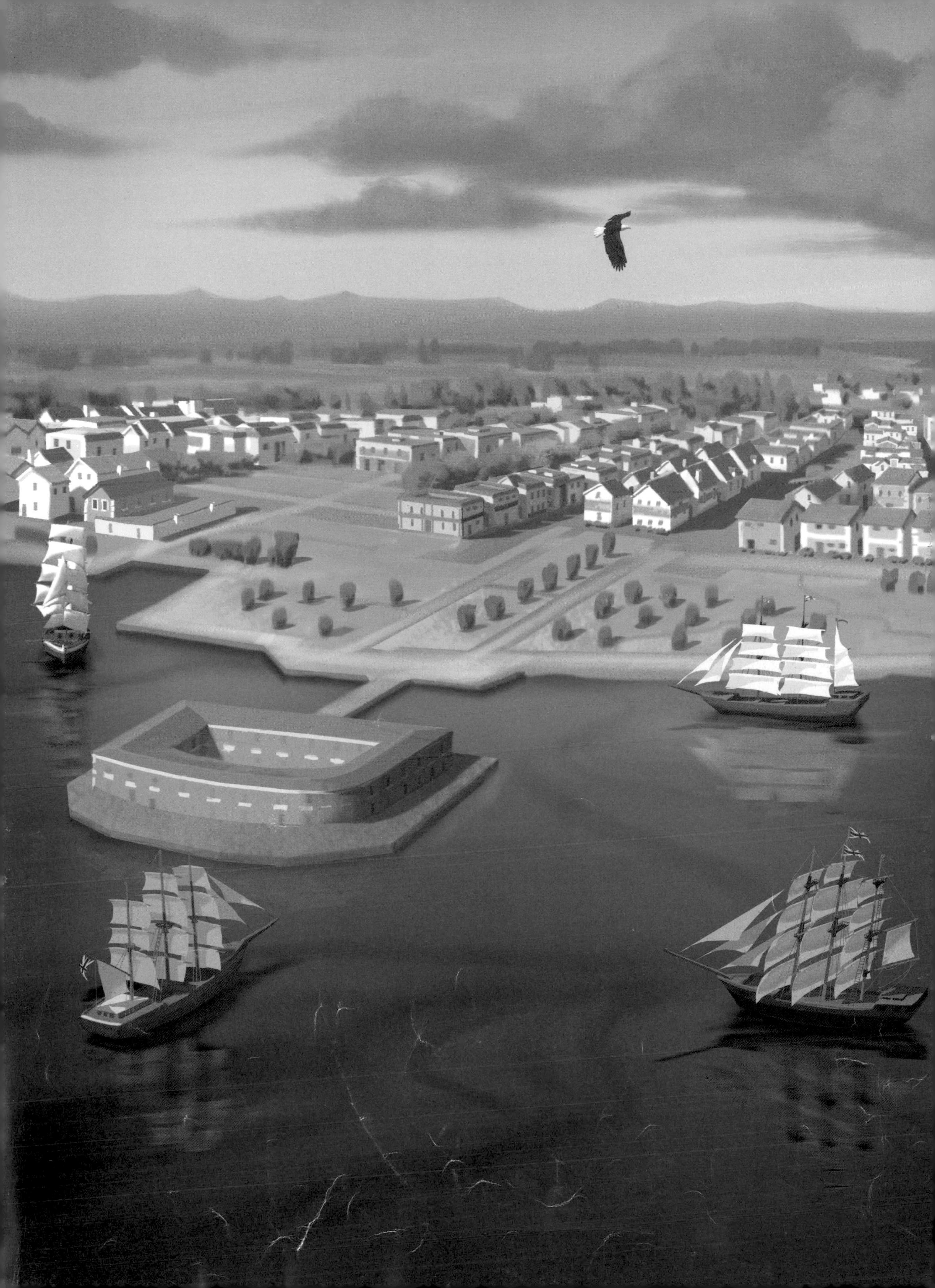

They wanted to leave behind the lives they led in a place they called the **Old World**

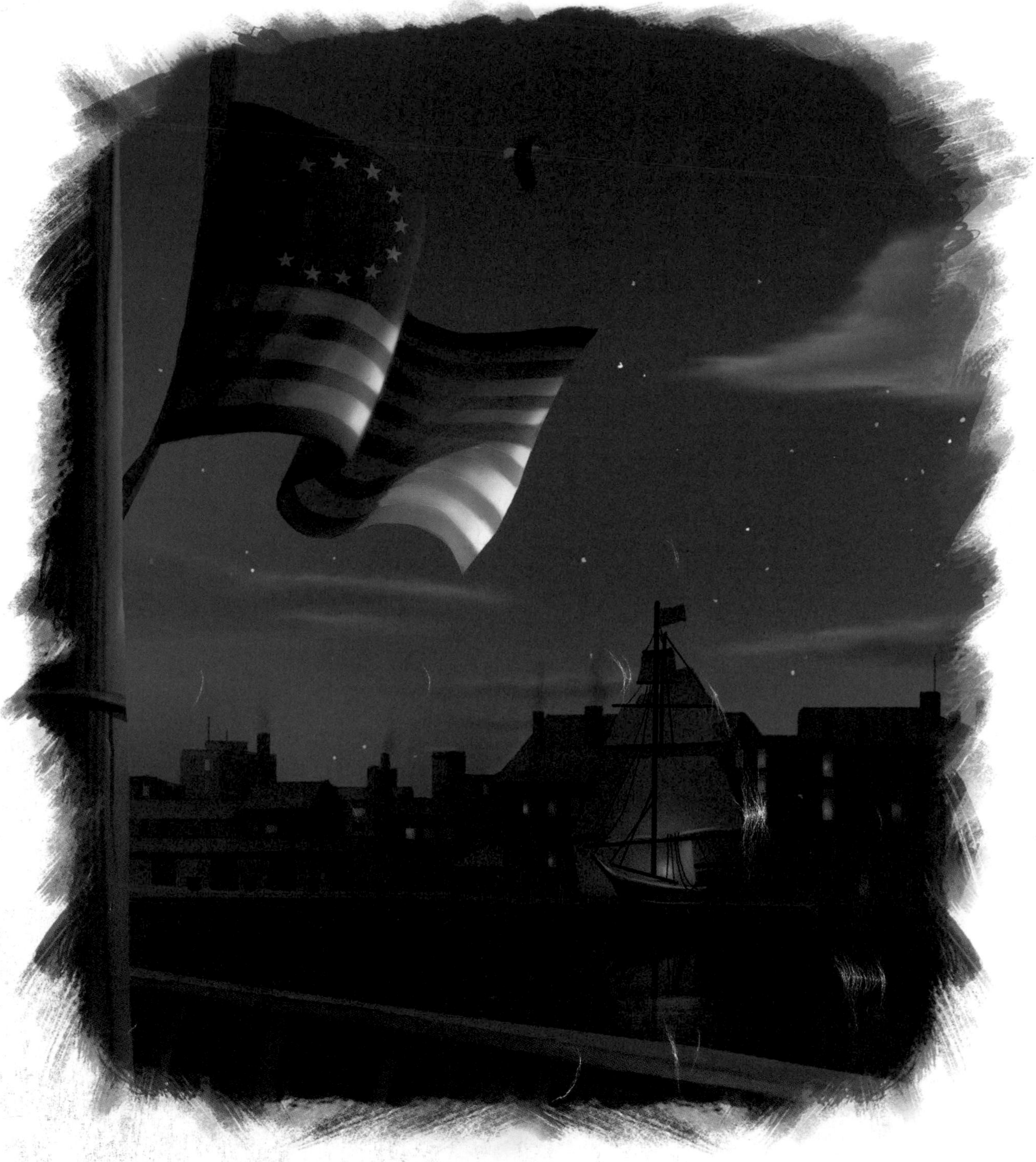

and build new ones in a place where they believed **anything was possible**.

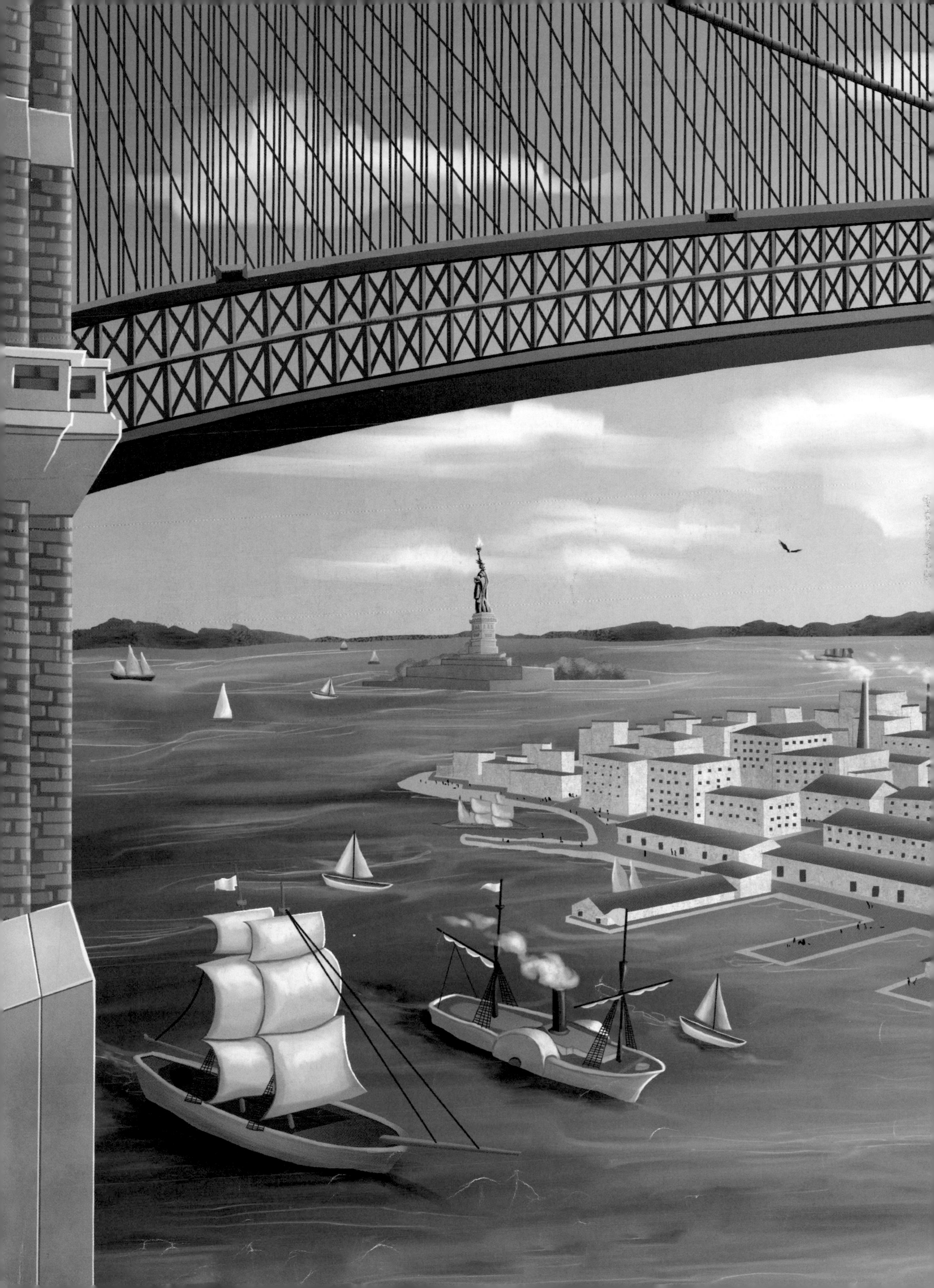

They came from all over the world.

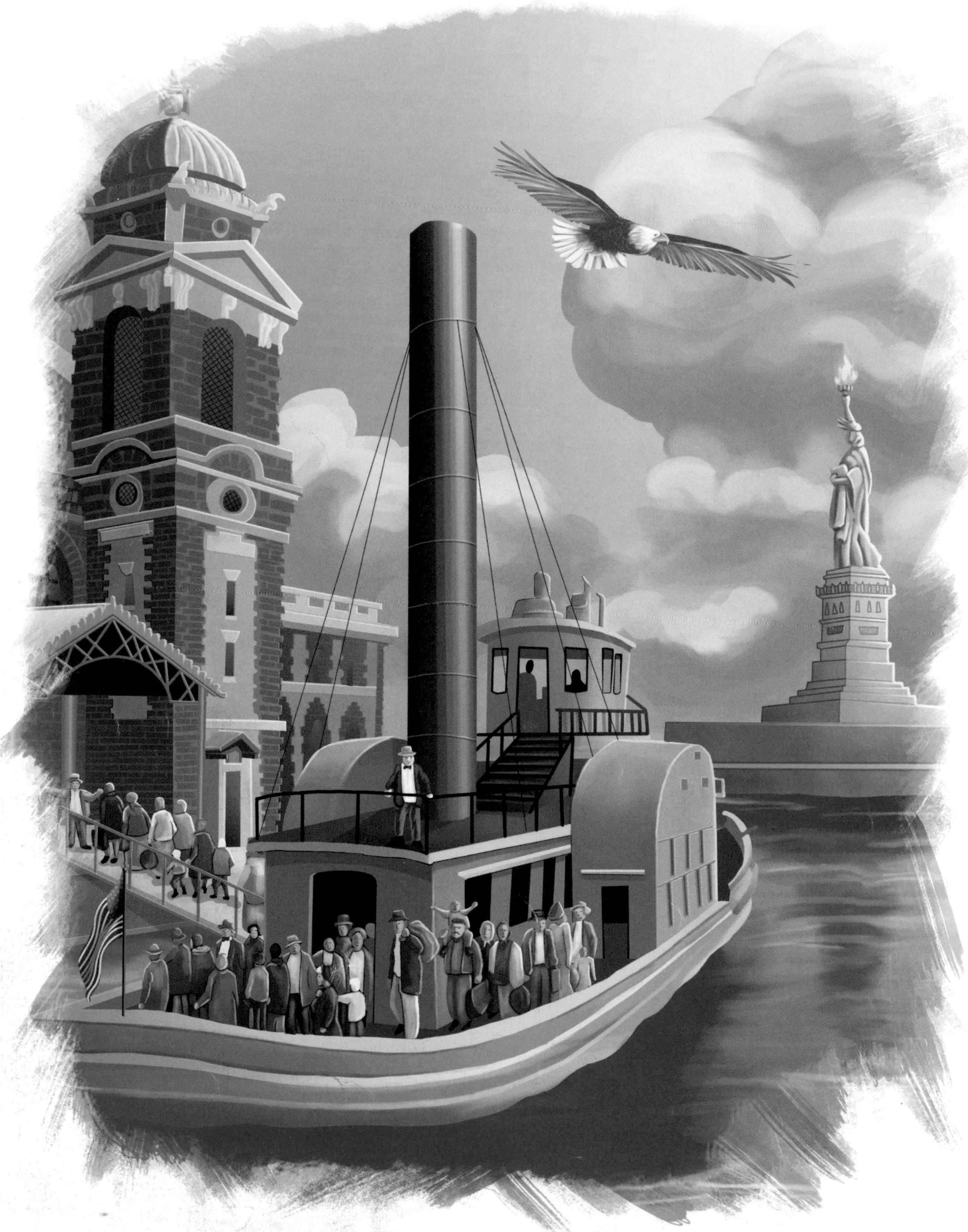

For most, this island was the first stop on the path to a new life in this young nation.

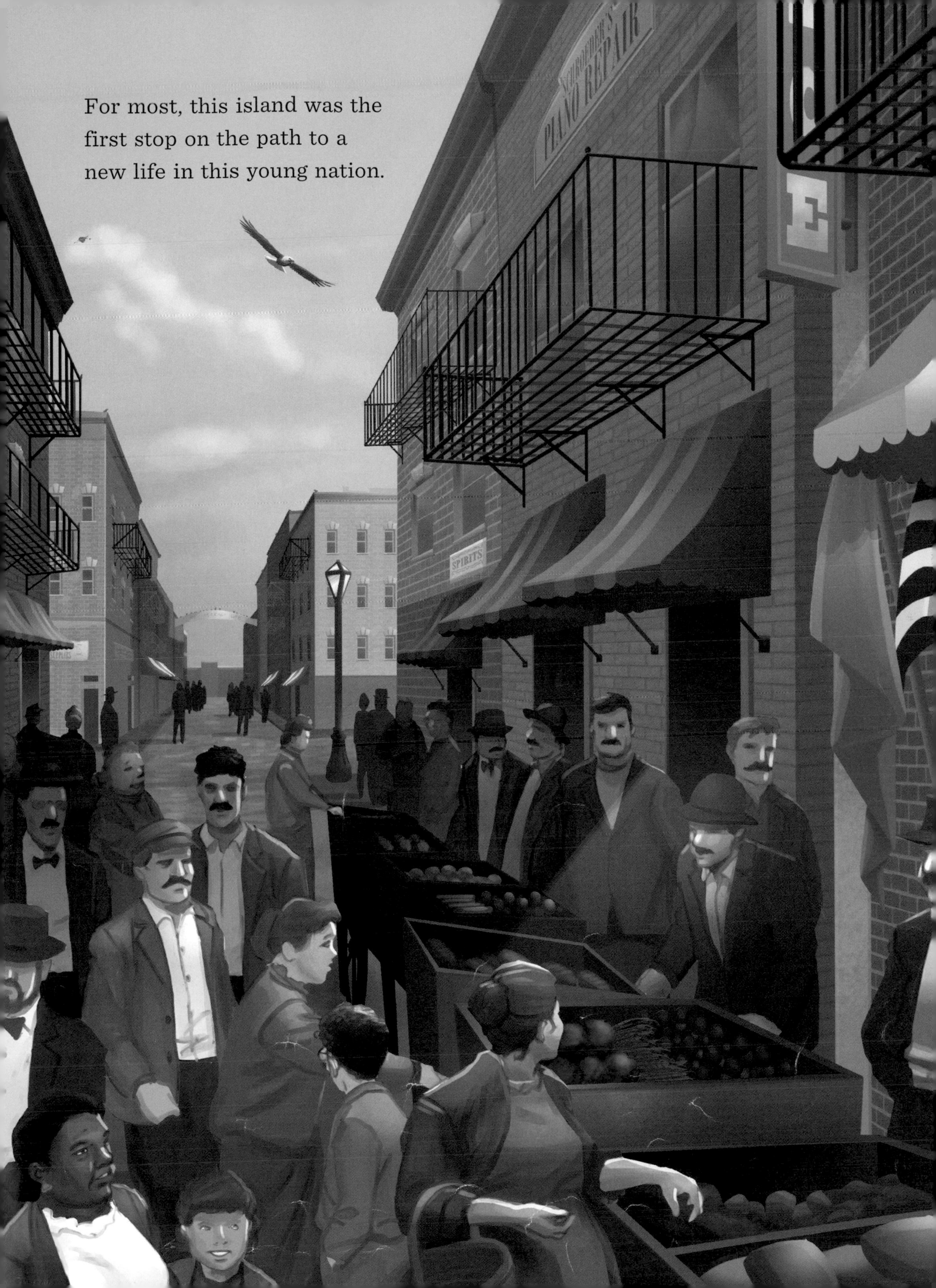
PIANO REPAIR
SPIRITS

This island was known as Manhattan,
in **the city of New York.**

The country would be known as
the United States of America—

or *America,* for short.

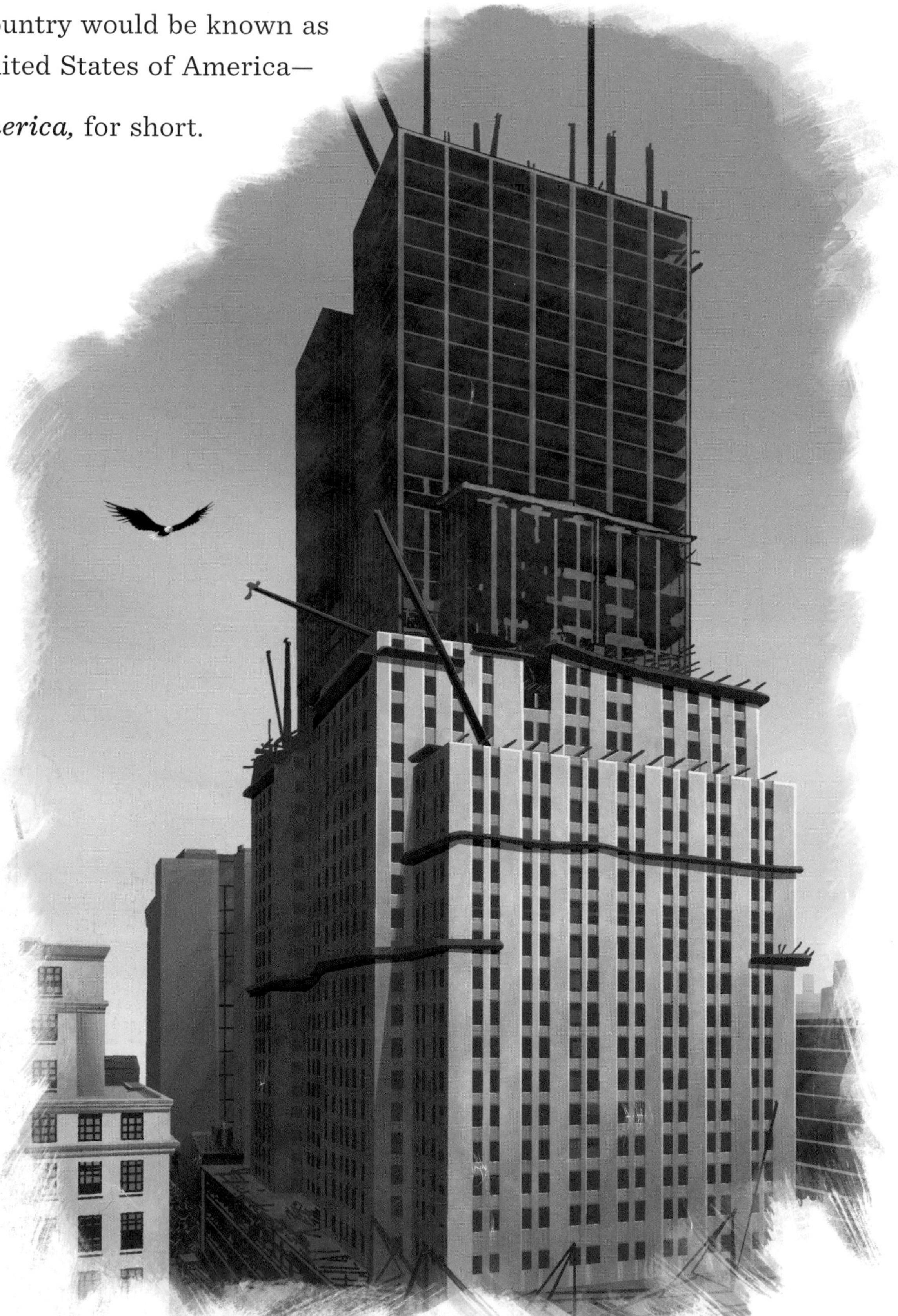

Before America was even two hundred years old,

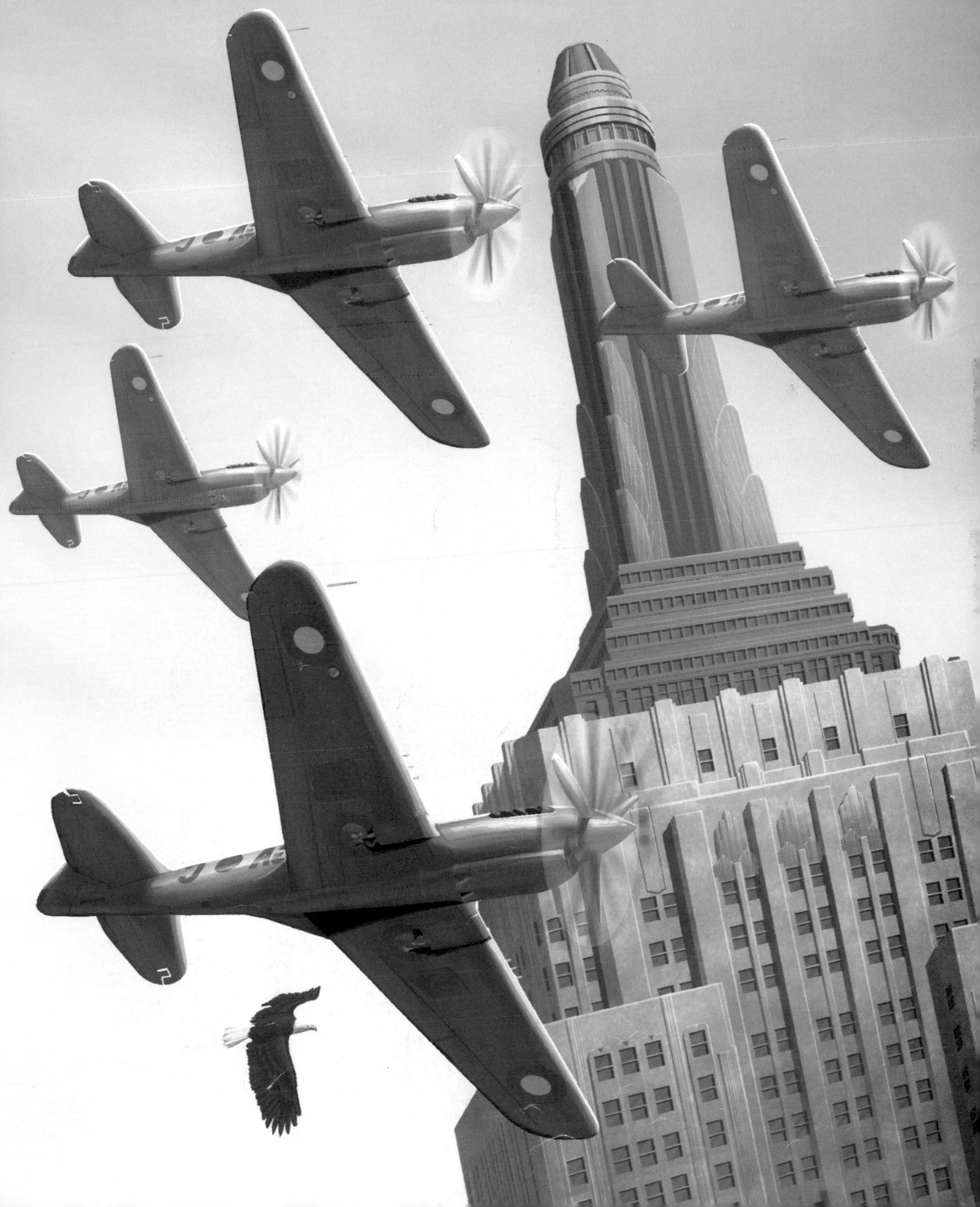

it was called upon to fight alongside other countries in a **terrible war** that was destroying the world.

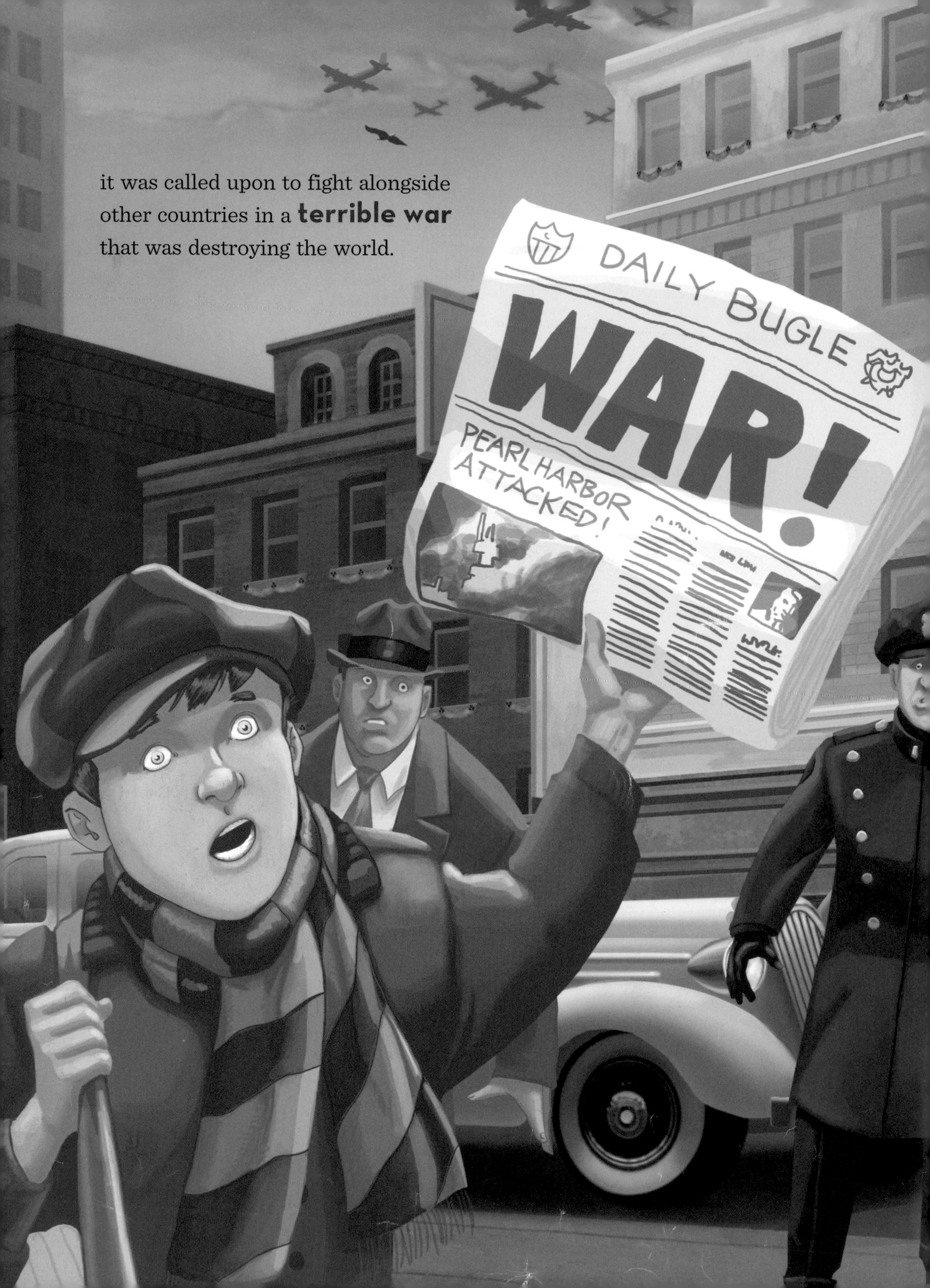
DAILY BUGLE
WAR!
PEARL HARBOR ATTACKED!

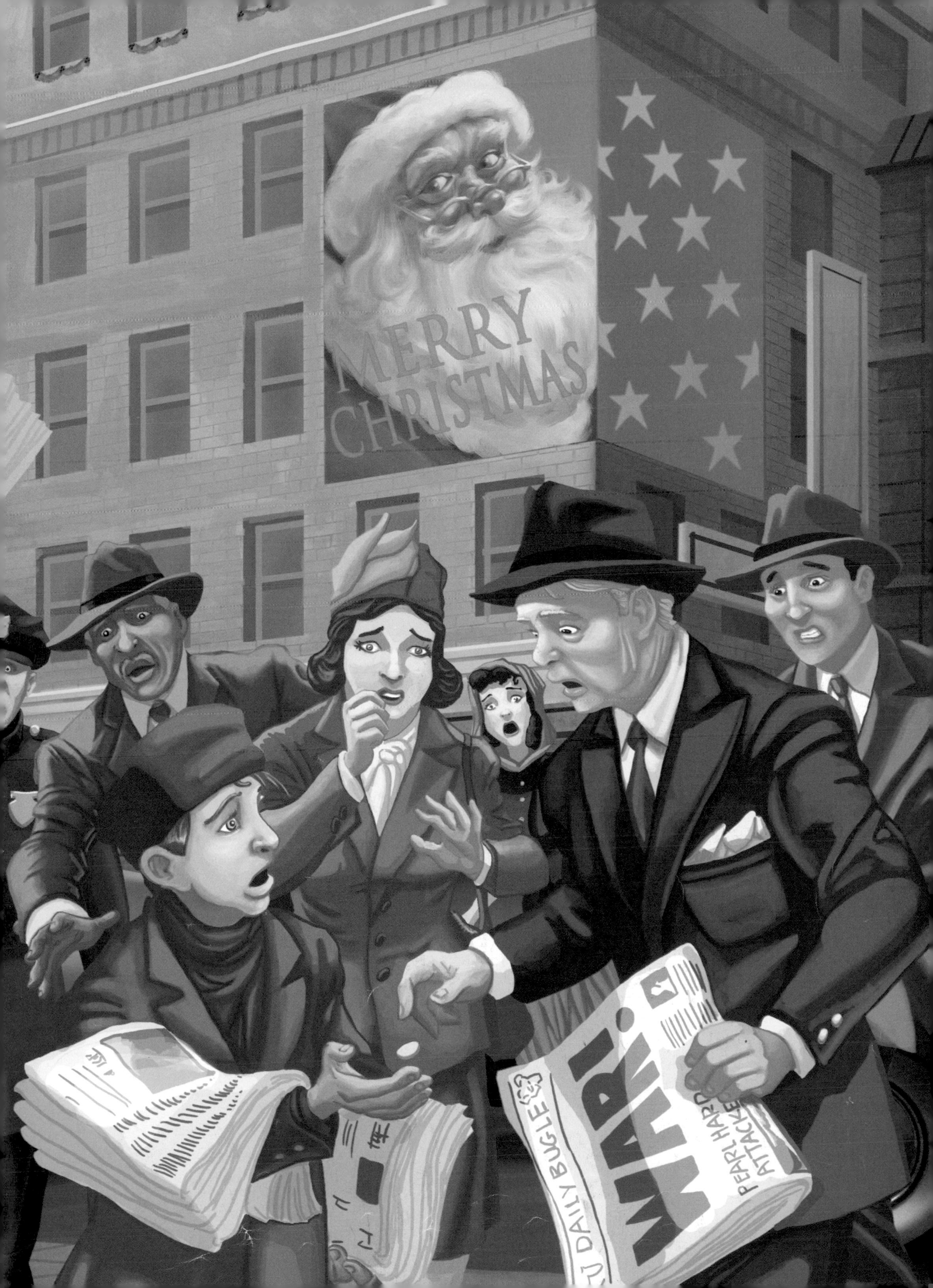
MERRY
CHRISTMAS
DAILY BUGLE
WAR!

The news of war moved people.

It seemed like everyone
in the country wanted
to join the army
to **help.**

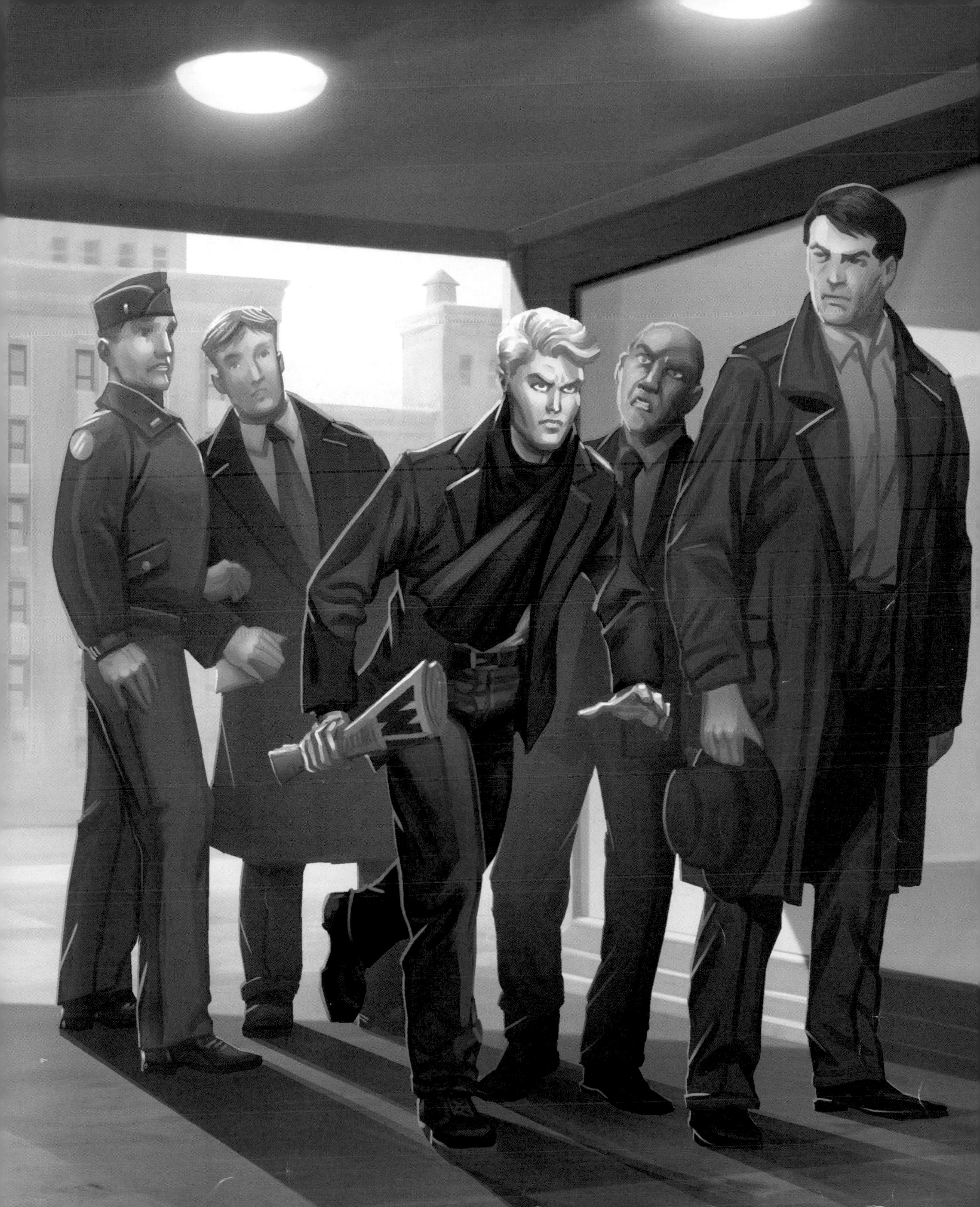

Including a young man named **Steve Rogers**.

Steve had been upset about the war for some time. Now that America was involved, he could **do something** about it.

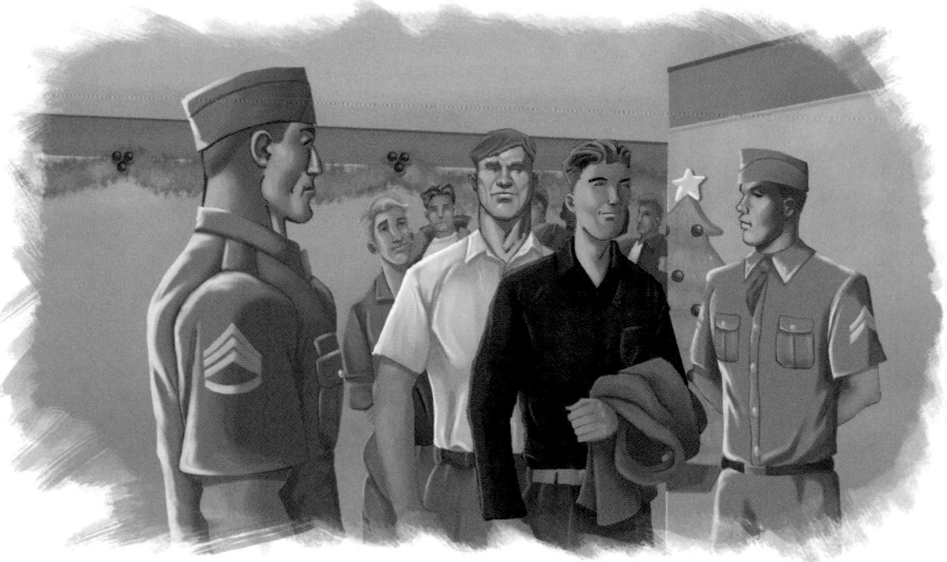

Soon, Steve was on a long line of men waiting to be examined. If the men passed, they would be deployed to the war.

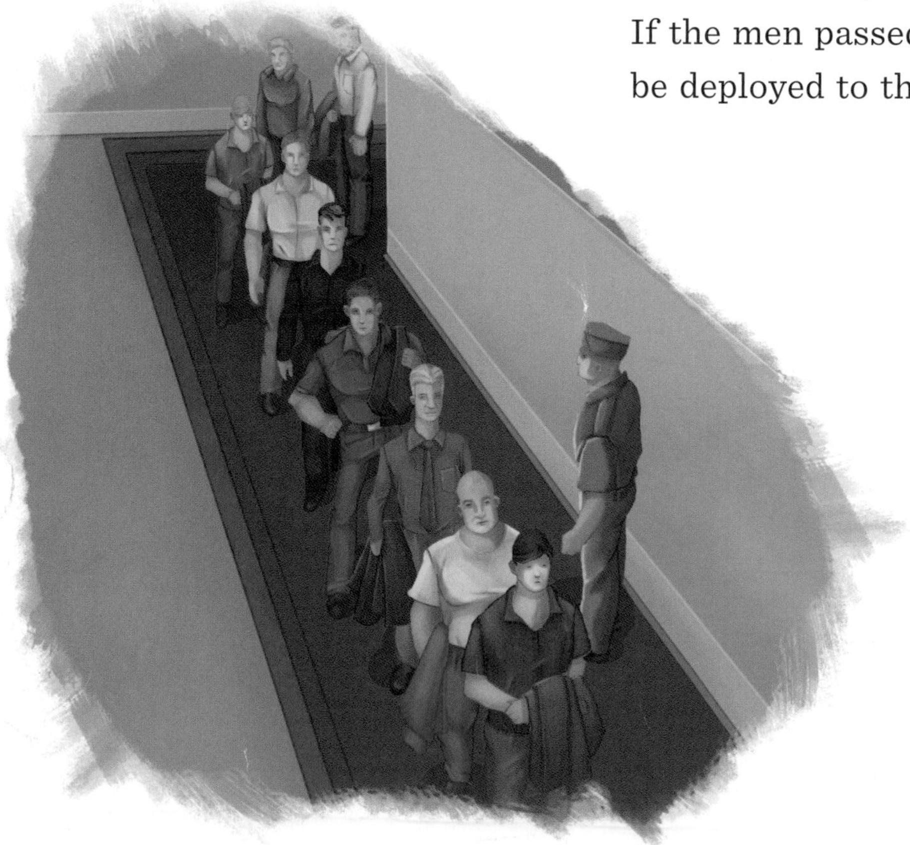

Steve waited his turn.

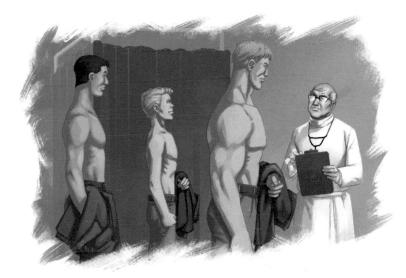

Every man so far had passed.

Steve was **confident** he would, too.

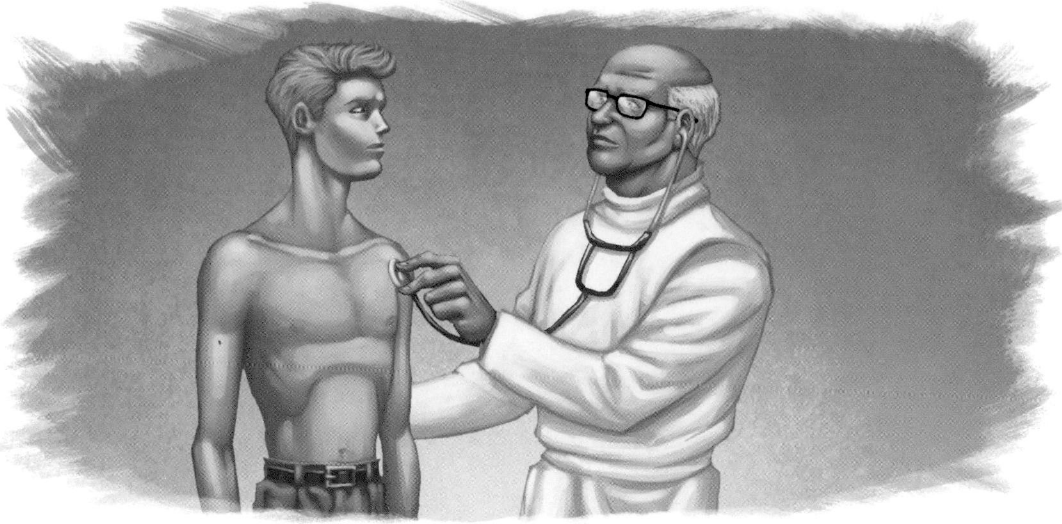

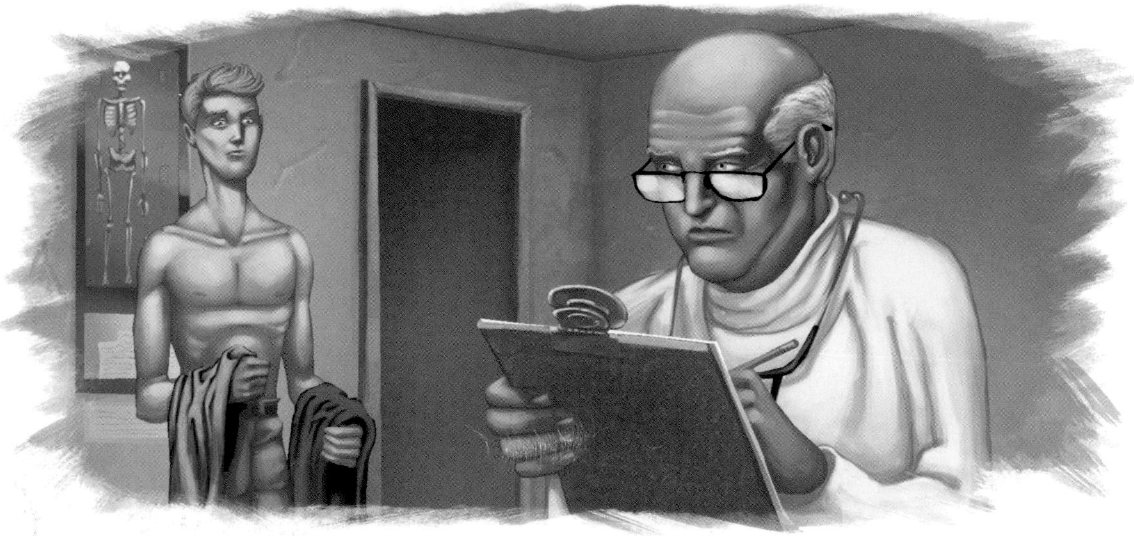

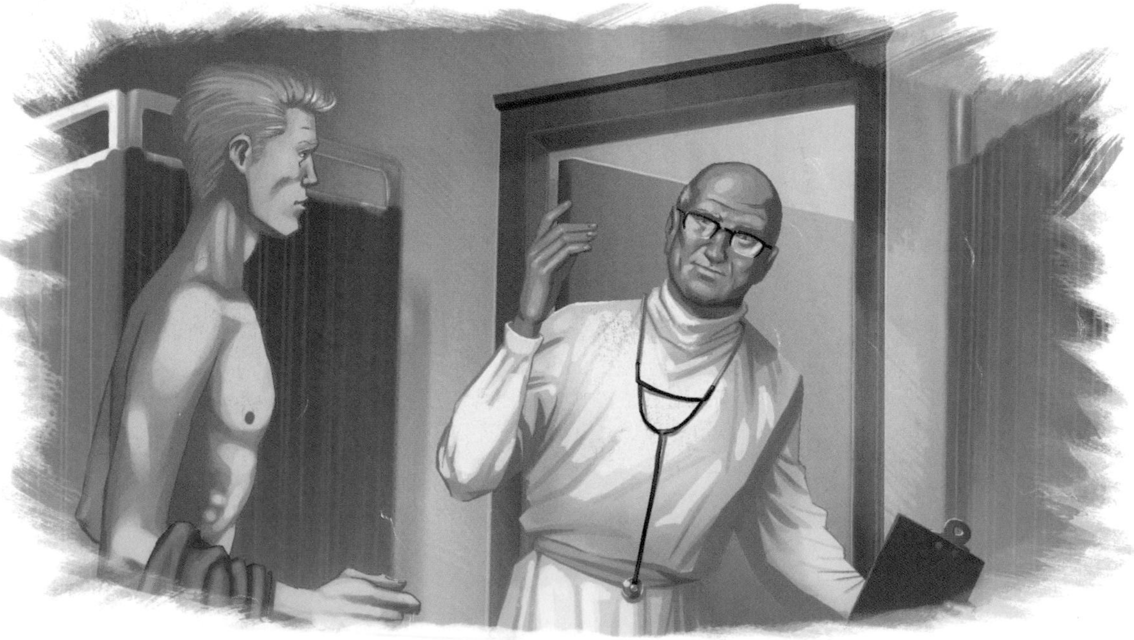

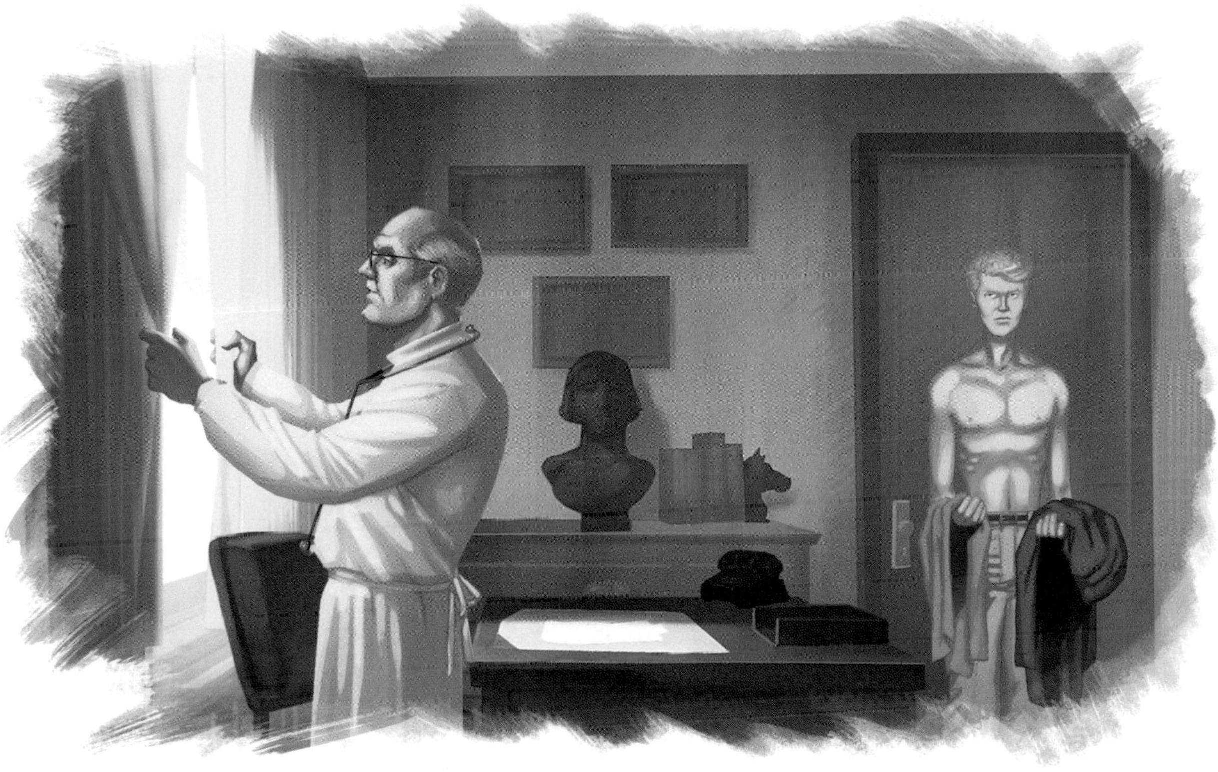

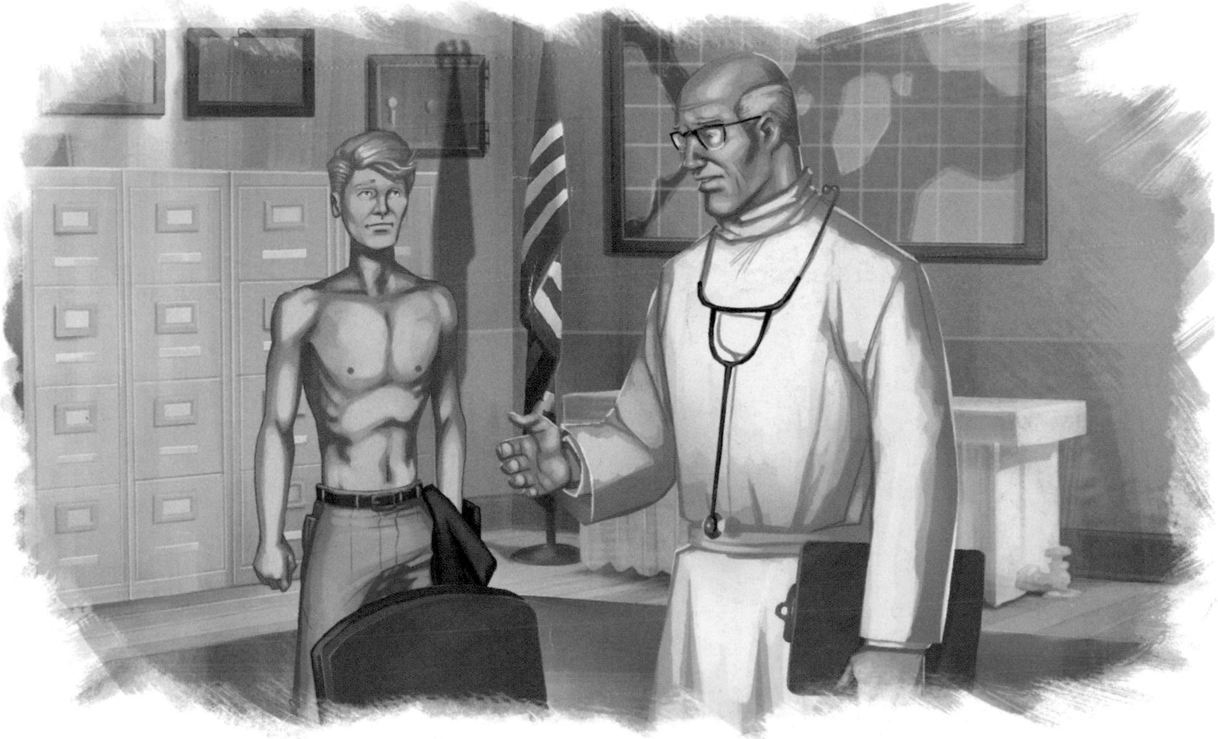

The doctor told Steve that he was in no shape to join the army.

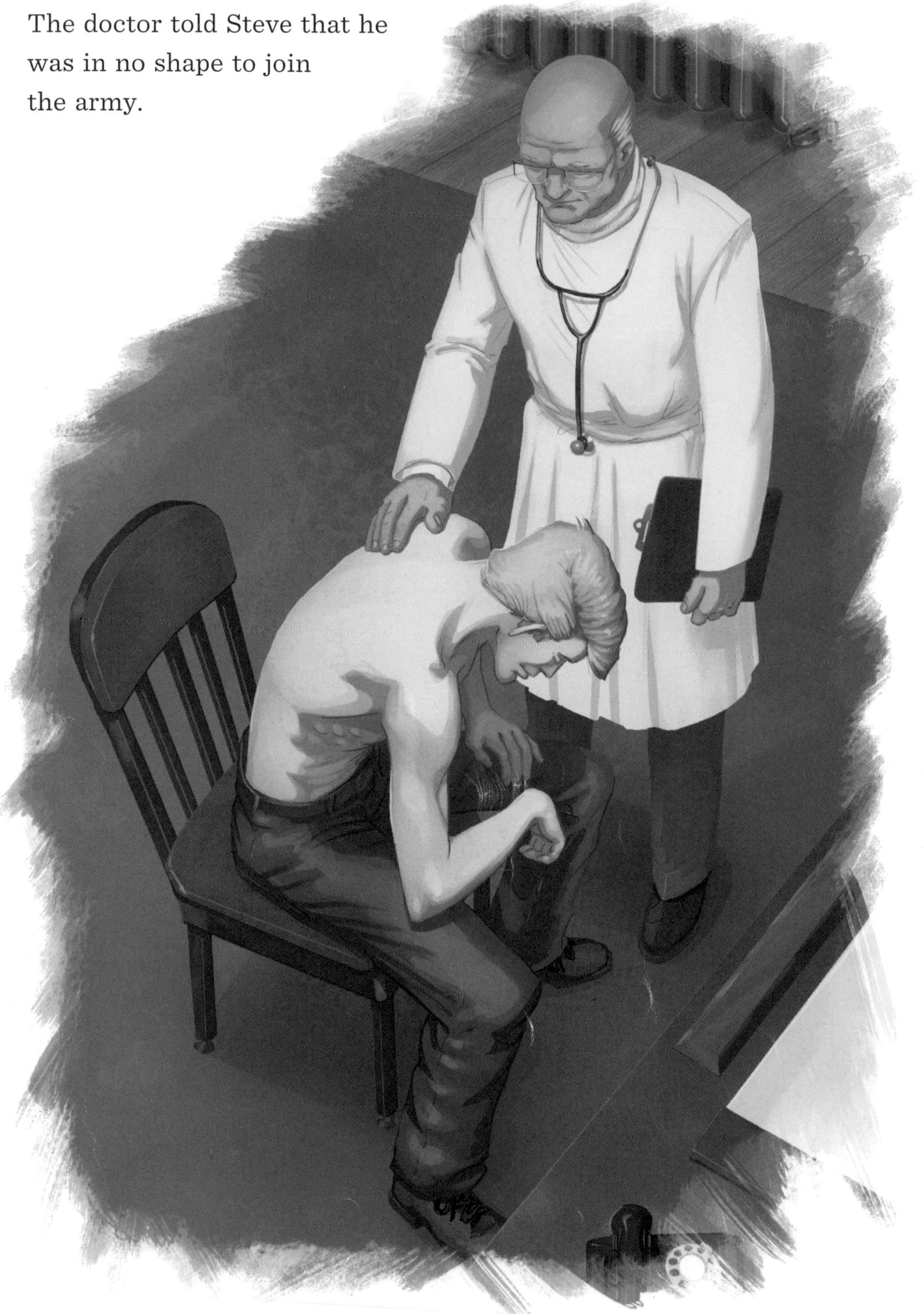

But then he told him there was another way to get into the army. He handed Steve a file marked

CLASSIFIED—PROJECT: REBIRTH.

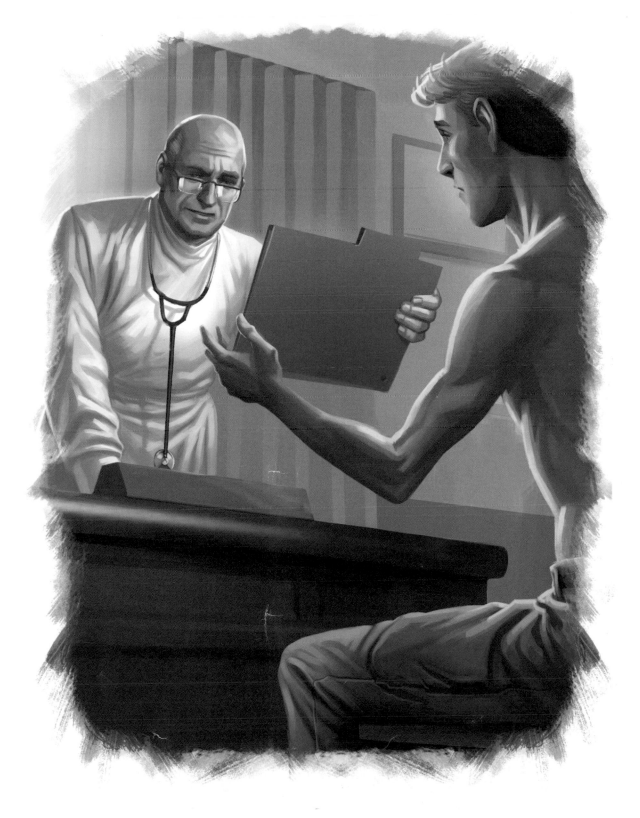

The doctor told Steve that if the experiment worked, he would be able to join the army.

Steve said he would try anything to become a soldier.

The doctor called in a general named **Chester Phillips**. General Phillips was in charge of Project: Rebirth.

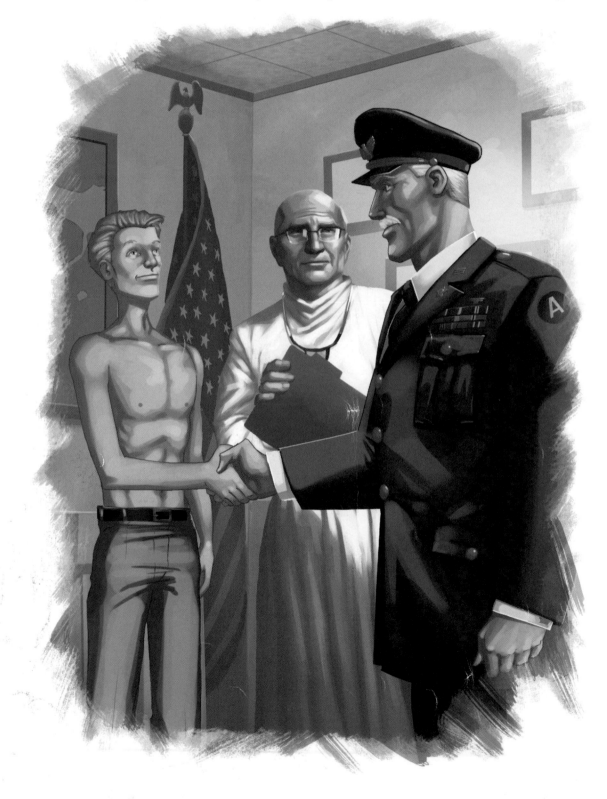

The general led Steve down a **hidden hallway** to a secret exit.

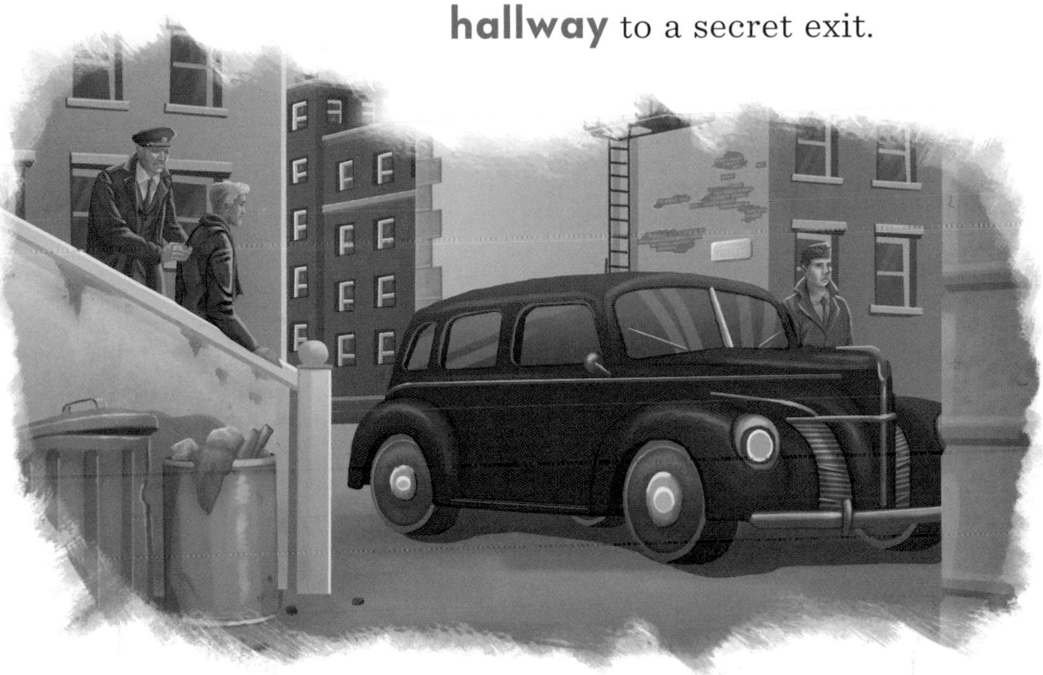

Soon the two men were crossing the bridge into nearby Brooklyn.

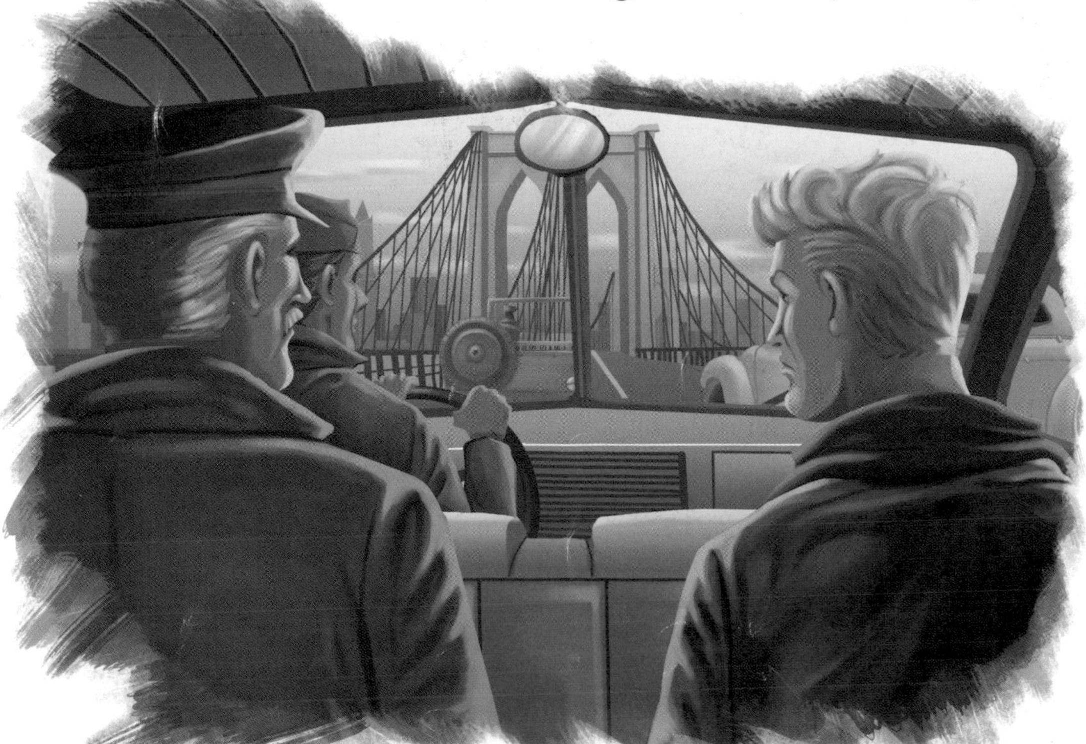

They arrived at an antiques
shop in a run-down,
dangerous-looking area.

An **old woman** let them in
and led them downstairs.

But the storefront was not an antiques shop at all!
It was a cover for an **underground lab**.

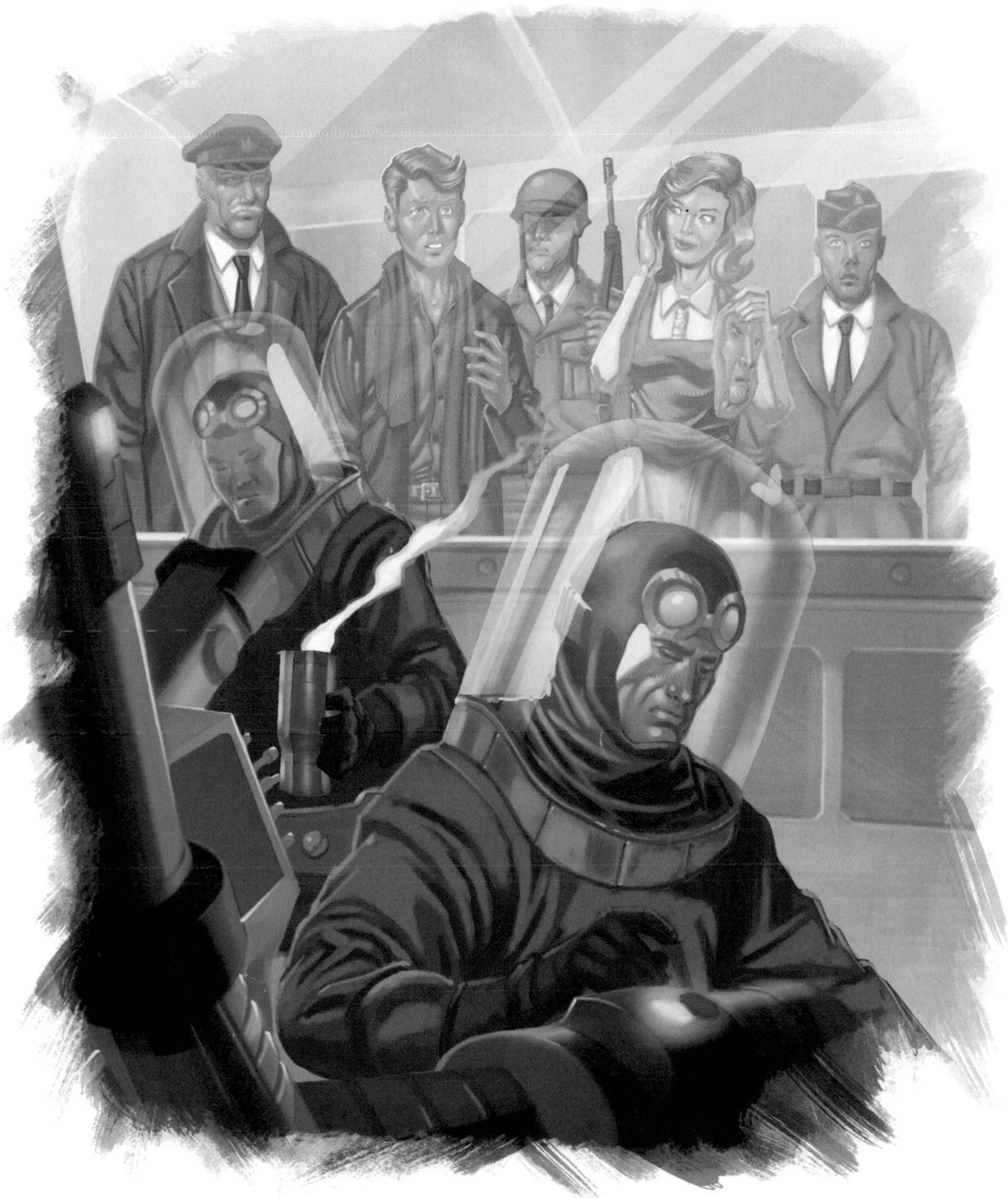

And the owner was not an old woman,
but a **secret agent!**

General Phillips introduced Steve to the project's lead scientist, **Doctor Erskine**.

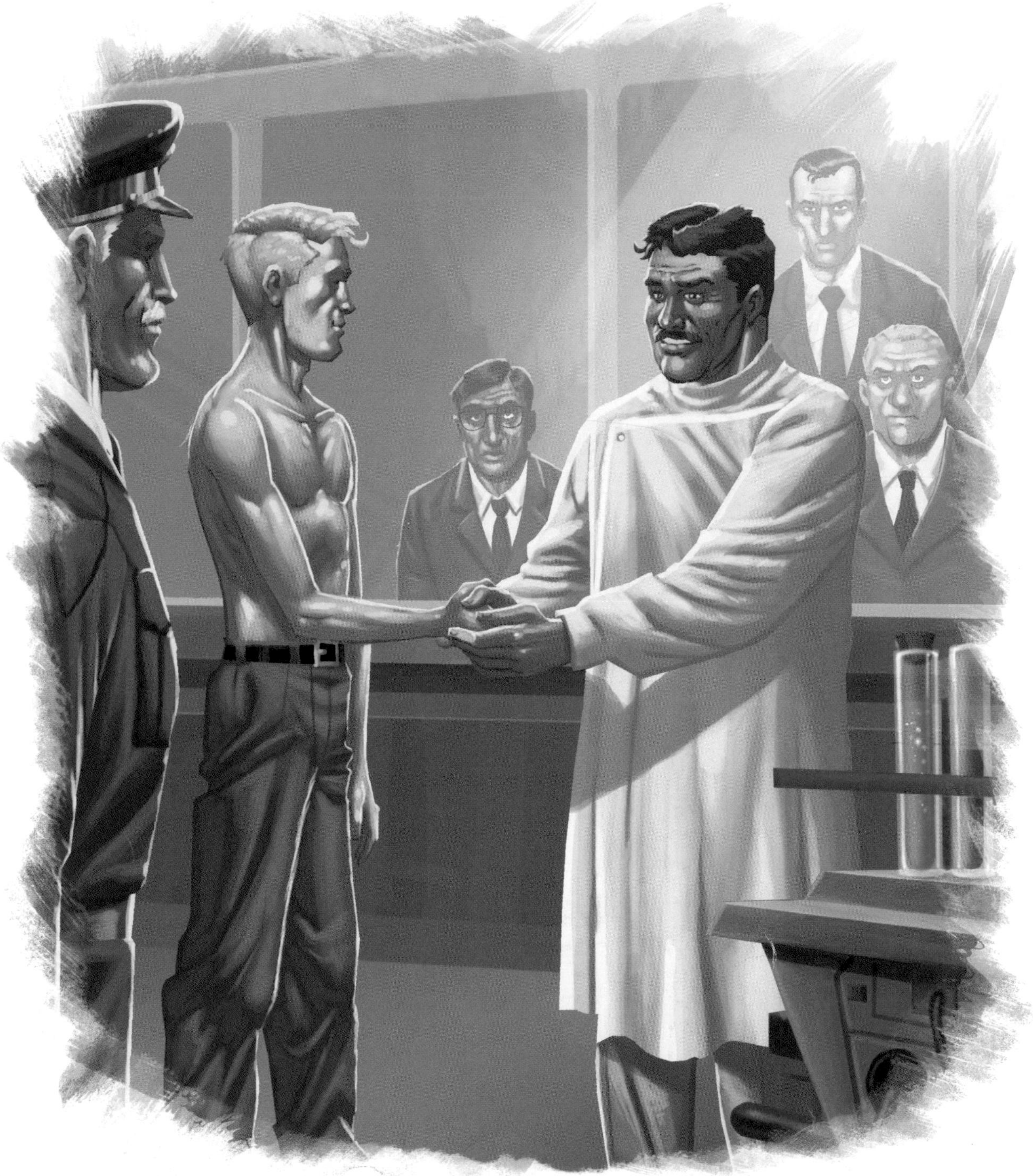

He told Steve that the **Super-Soldier serum** . . .

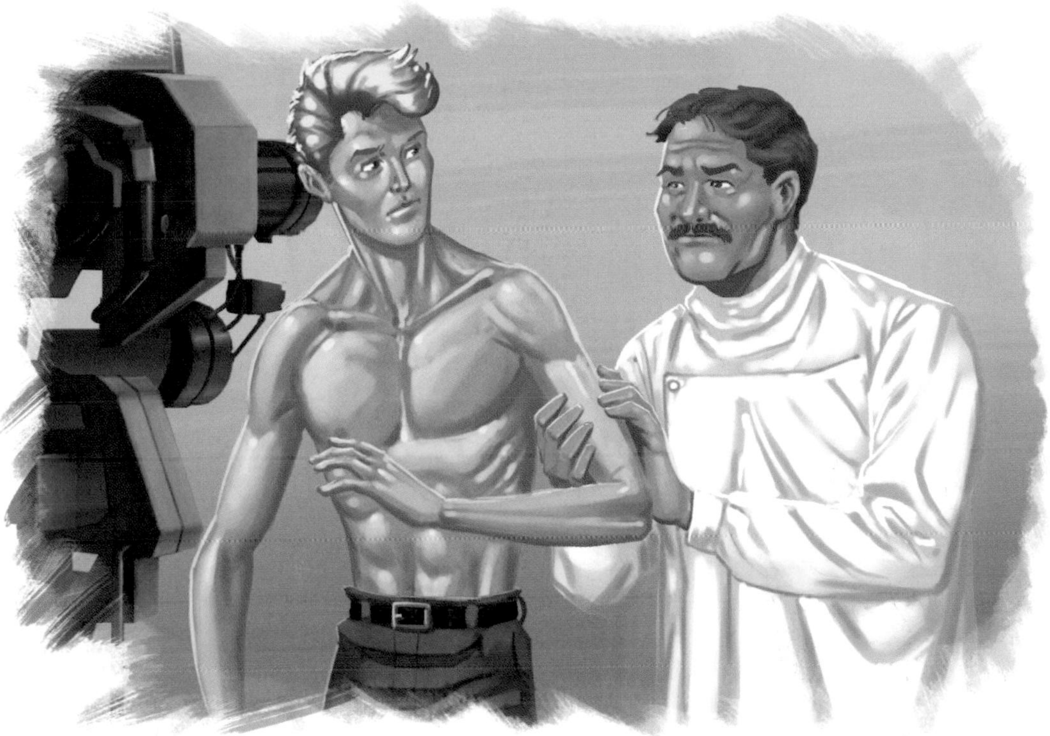

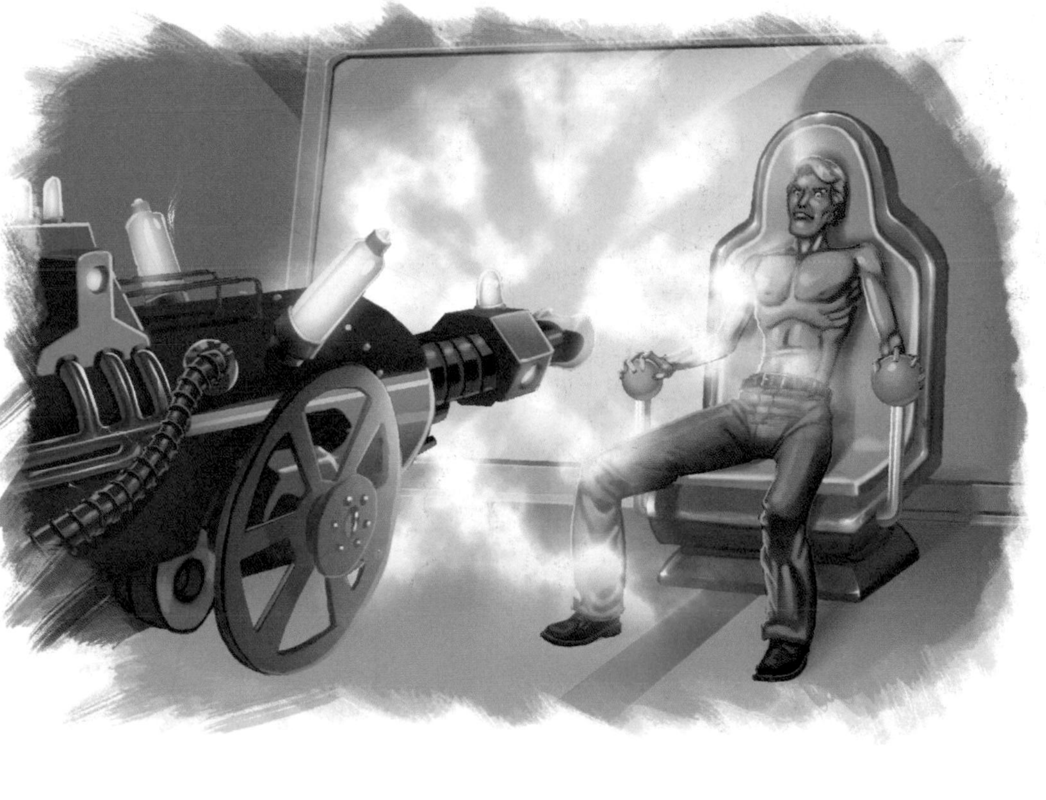

. . . combined with the **Vita-Rays** . . .

...would transform him
from frail and sickly...

...into America's

FIRST AVENGER!

The experiment was a

SUCCESS!

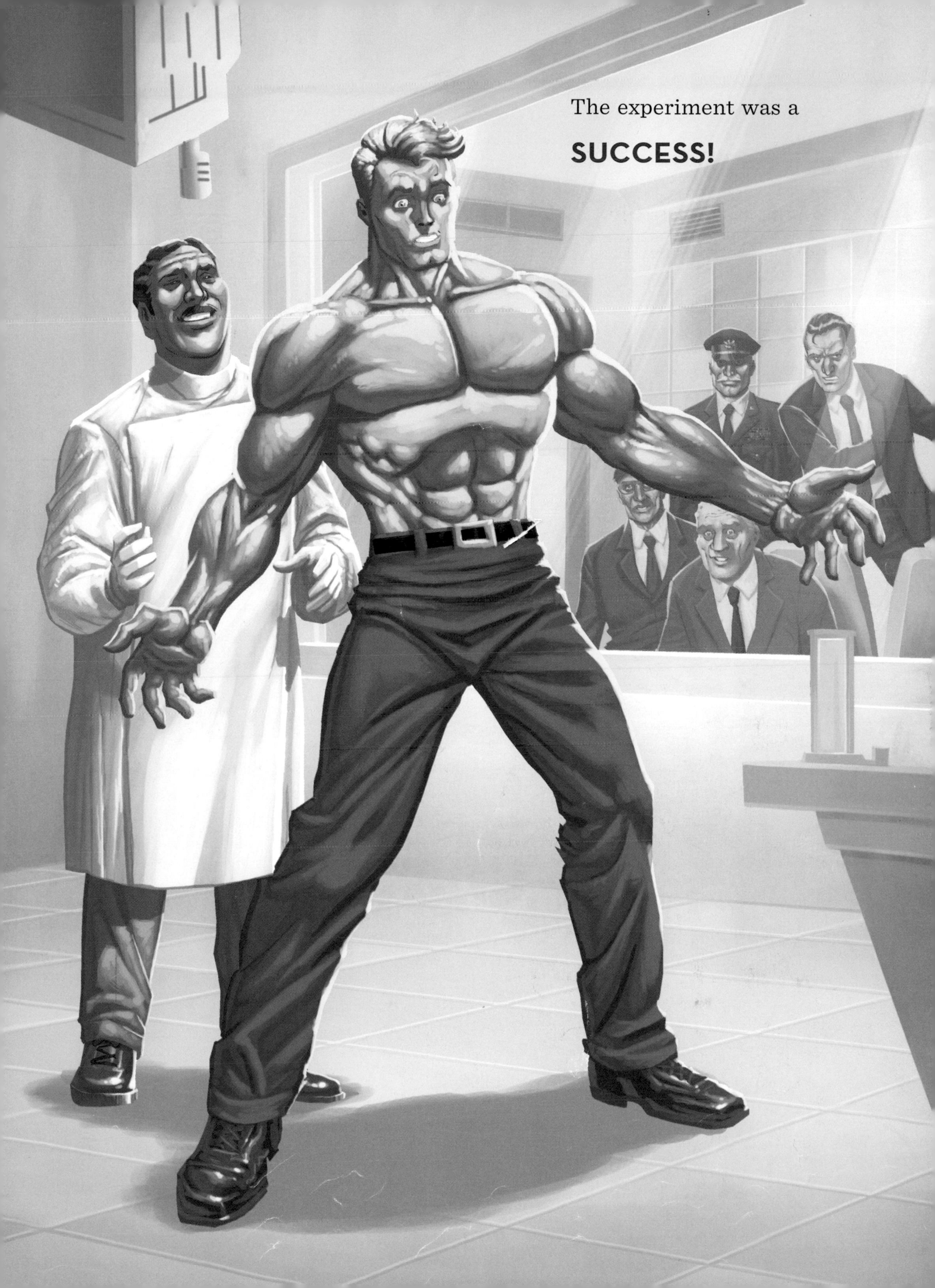

But before Steve, General Phillips, or anyone else in the lab could notice, an **enemy spy** who had been working in the lab attacked!

He did not want the Americans to have such power!

The doctor was hurt and unable to duplicate the serum.

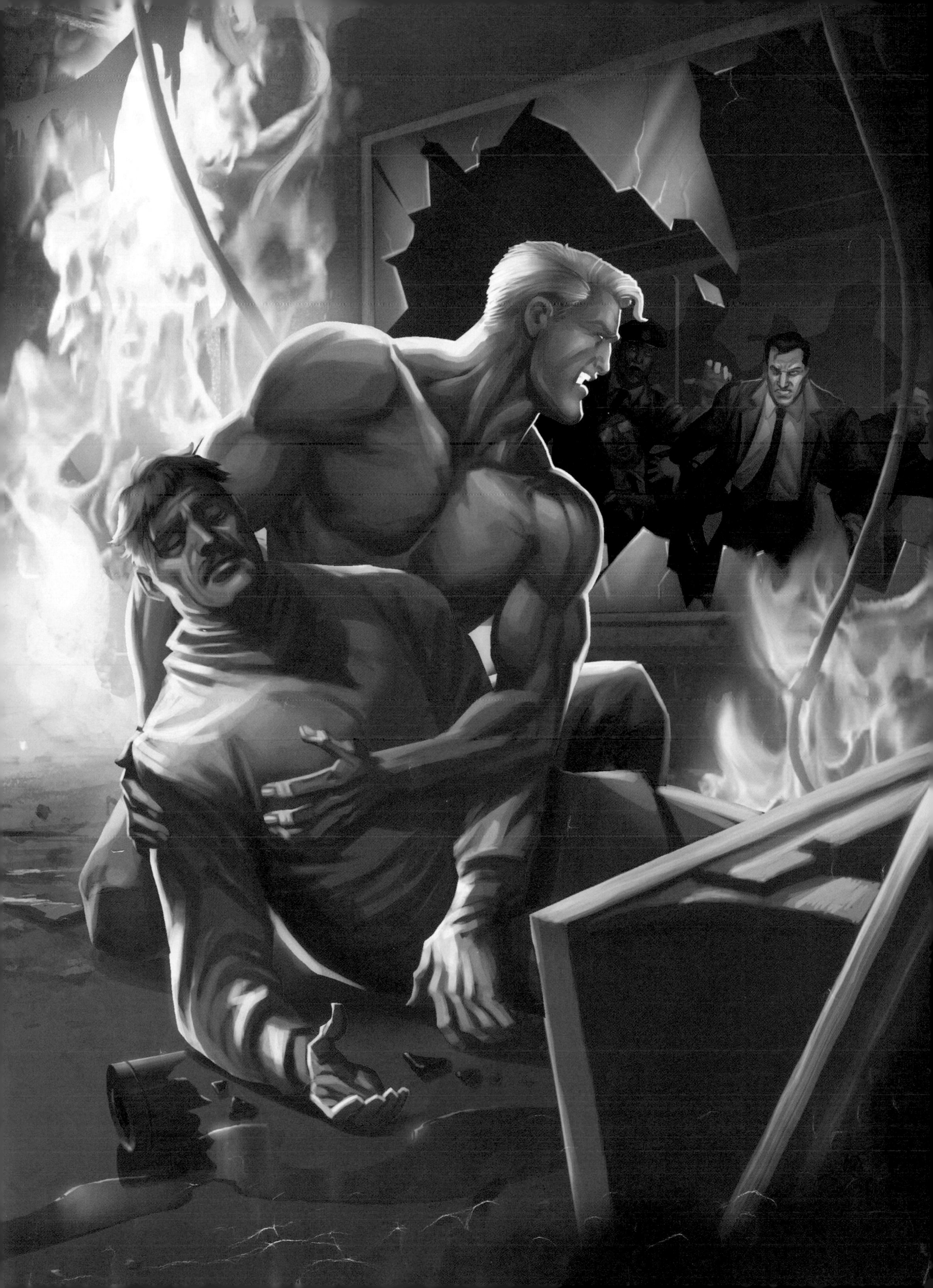

But Steve, in his new
Super-Soldier body,
was safe.

**AND HE WAS
ANGRY!**

The army put Steve through a very special training camp to teach him how to use his new body.

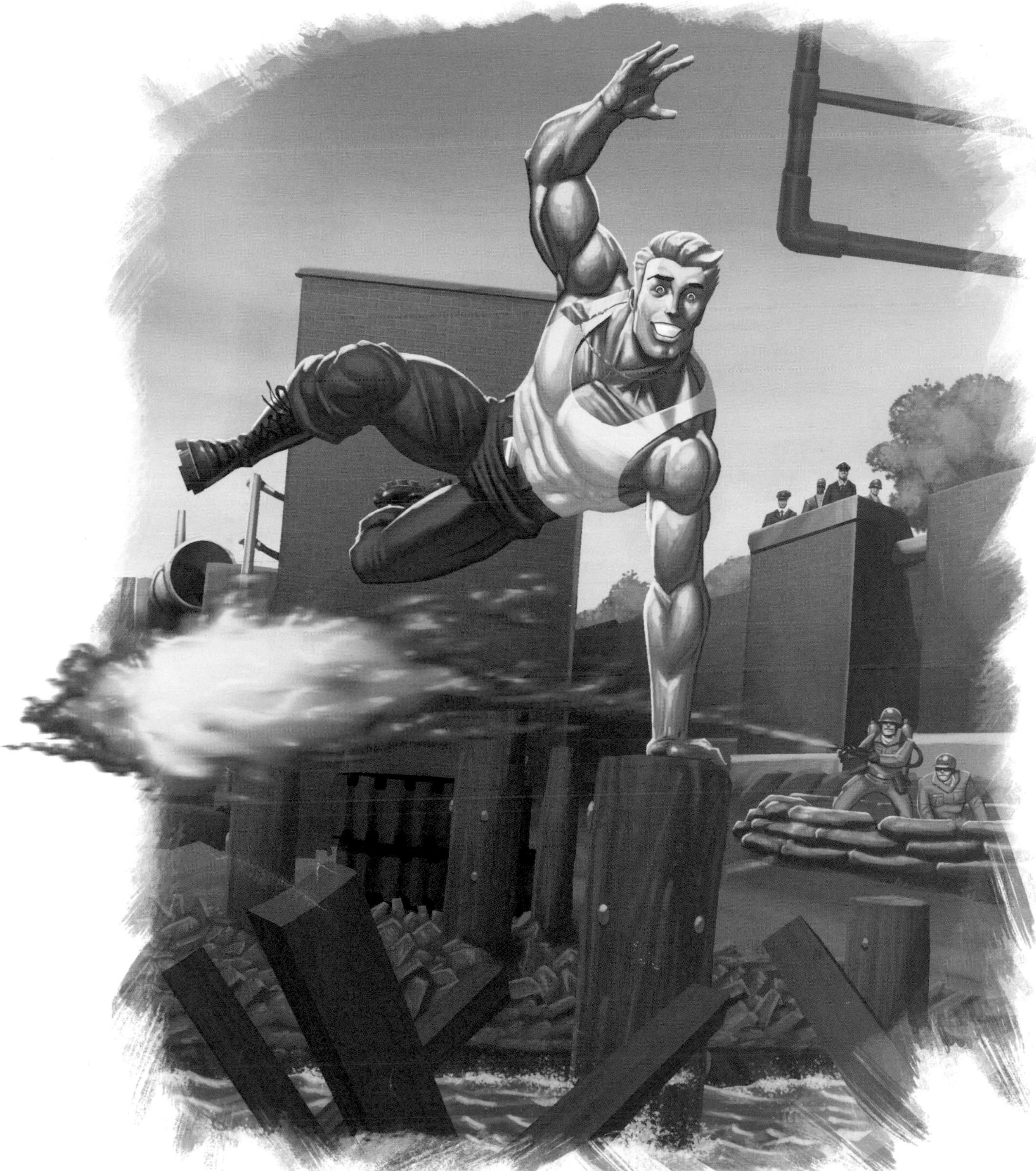

The general presented Steve with a **special shield** made of the strongest metal known and a **unique costume** to help Steve mask his identity.

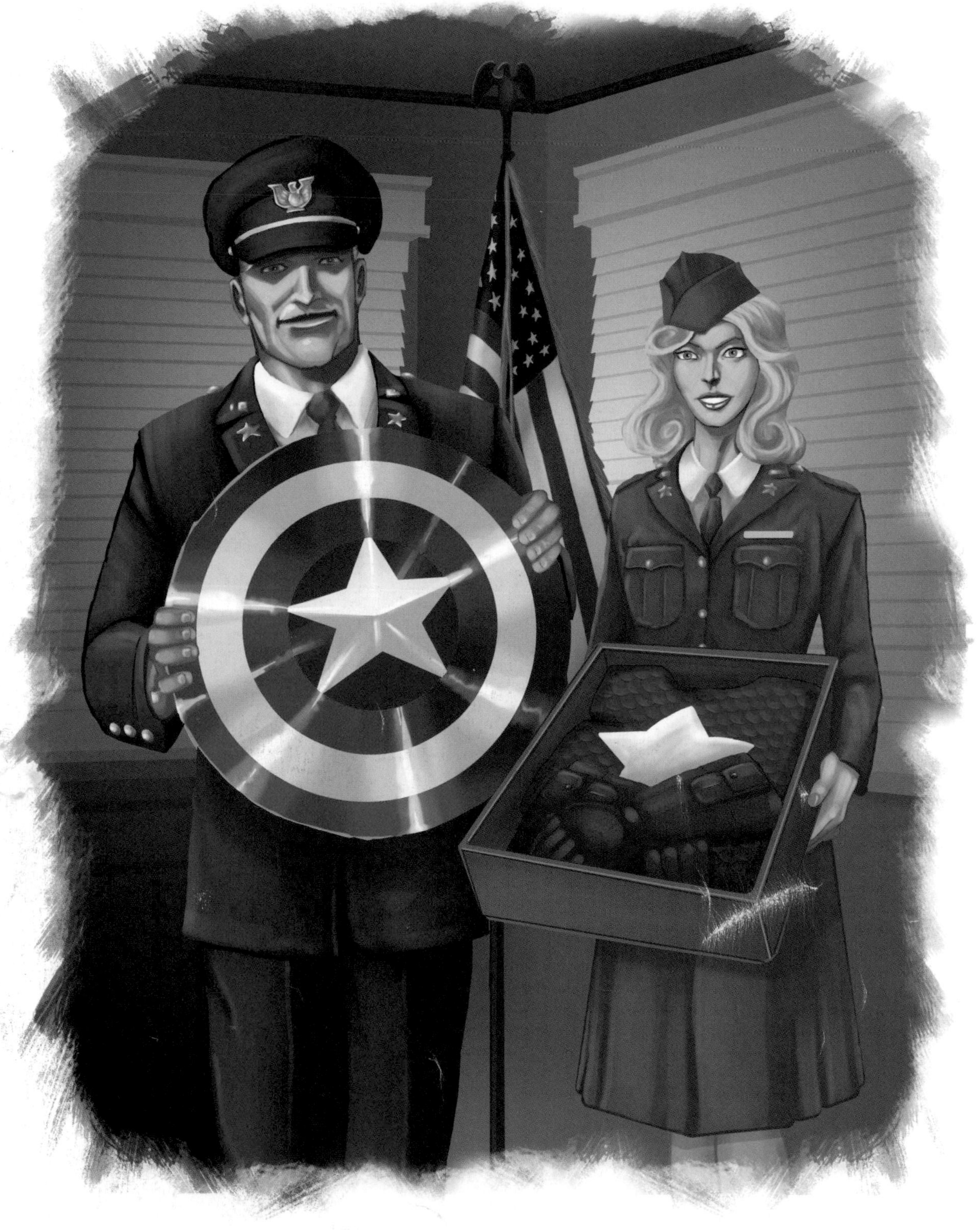

With the costume and shield, Steve would now be known as America's most powerful soldier . . .

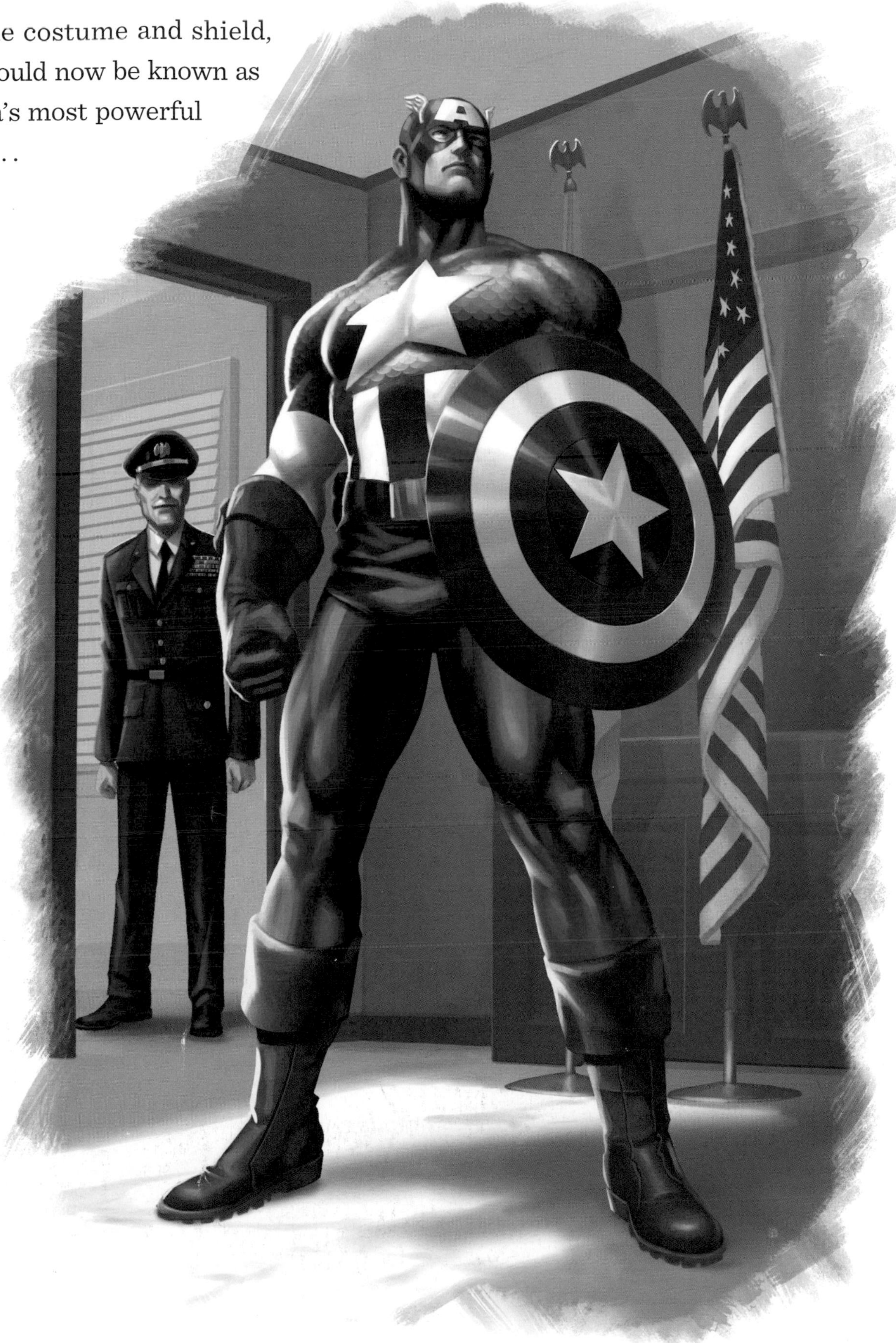

CAPTAIN AMERICA!

Captain America's missions were often **dangerous**.

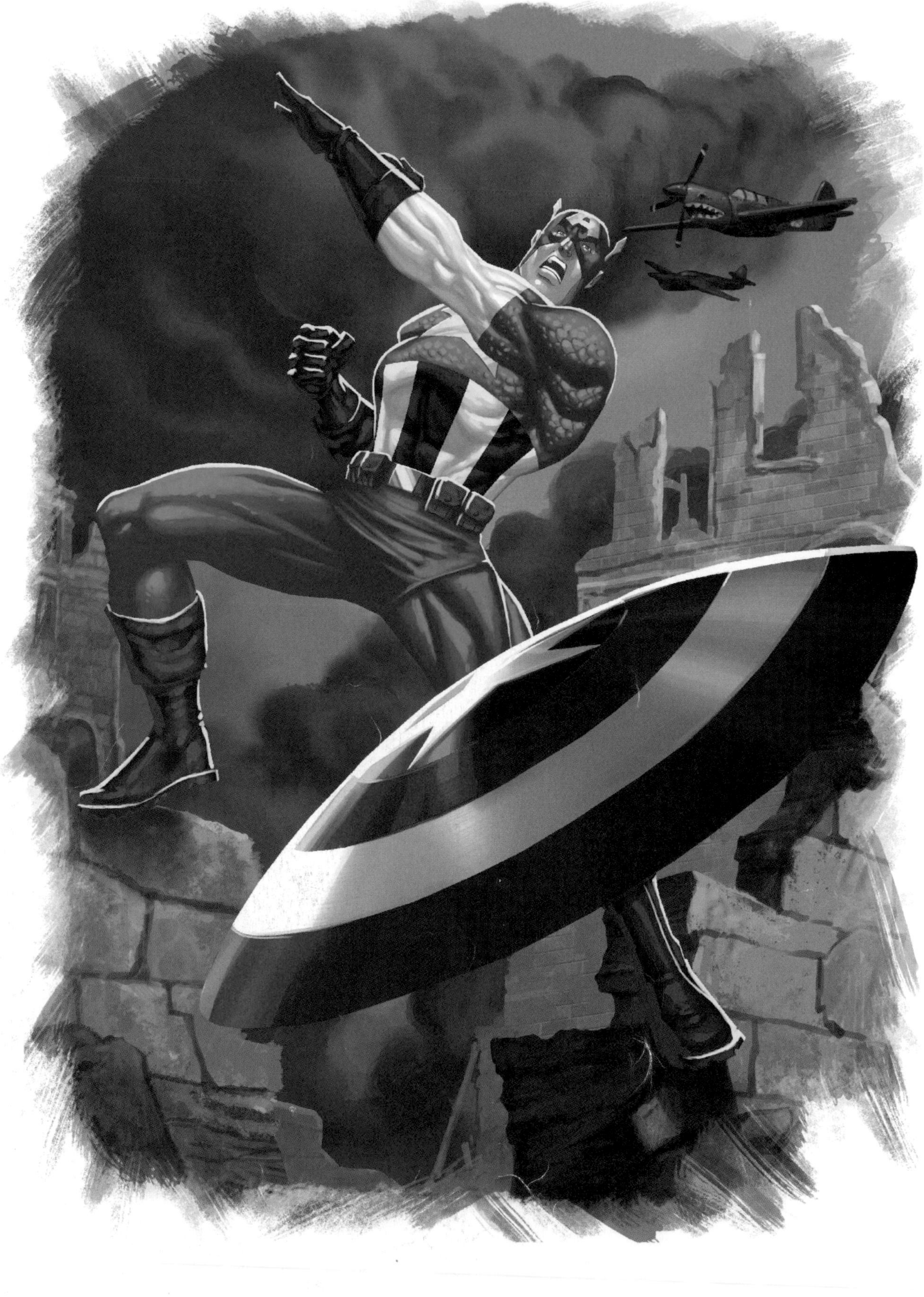

In order to keep his secret safe, the general asked Steve to pretend to be a **clumsy** army private.

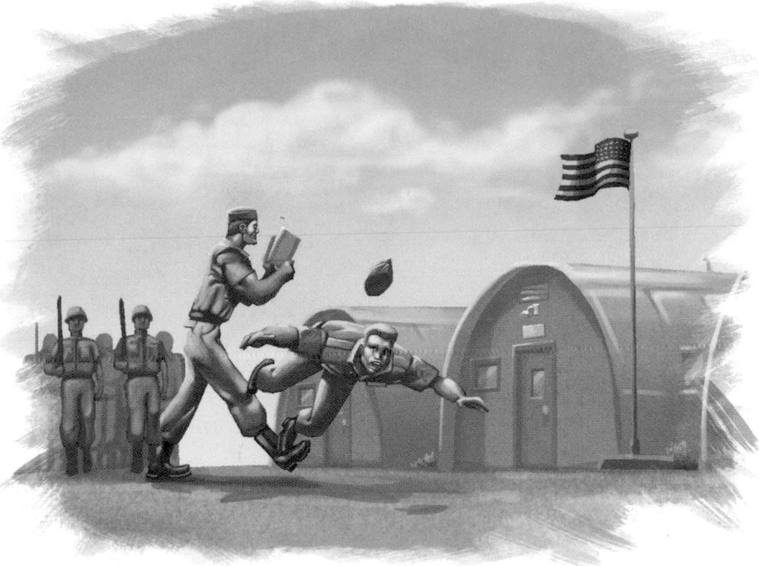

But when no one was looking, Steve donned his costume and fought for **justice**.

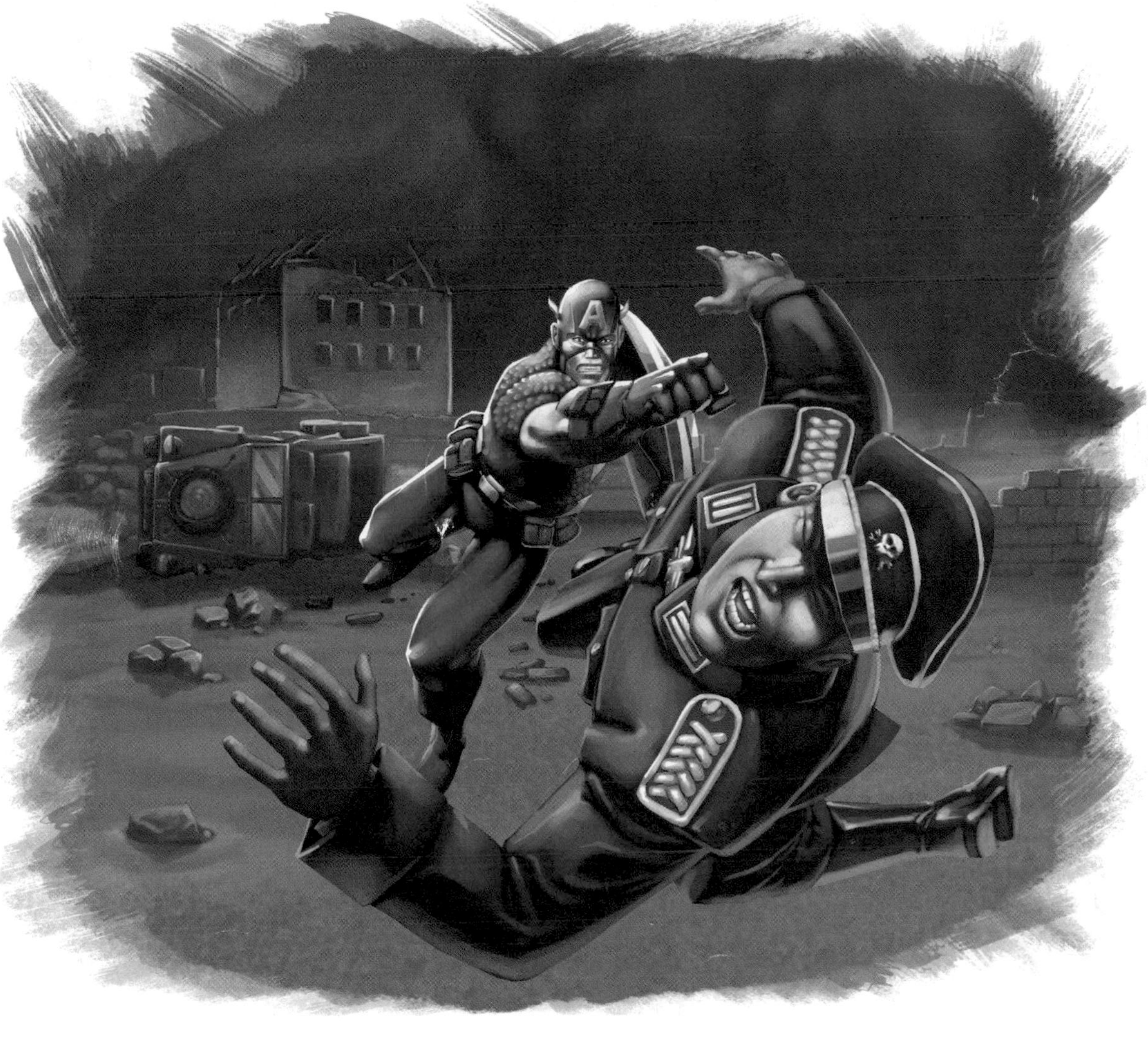

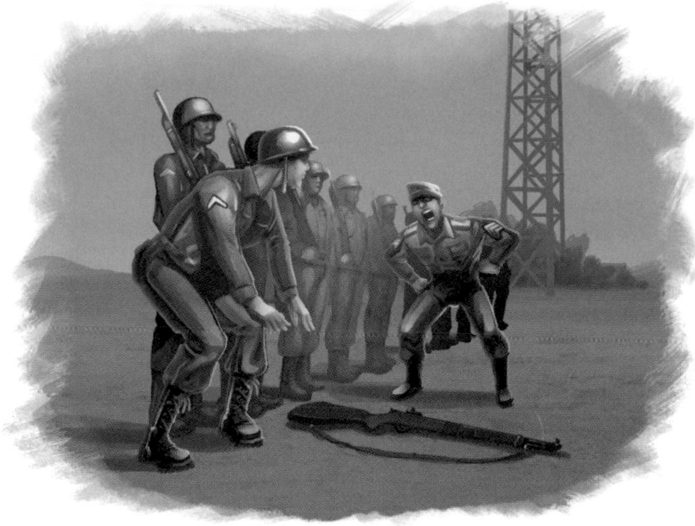

Steve's reputation as a klutz meant he was transferred often.

But Steve's moving around allowed **Captain America** to fight on many different fronts of the worldwide war!

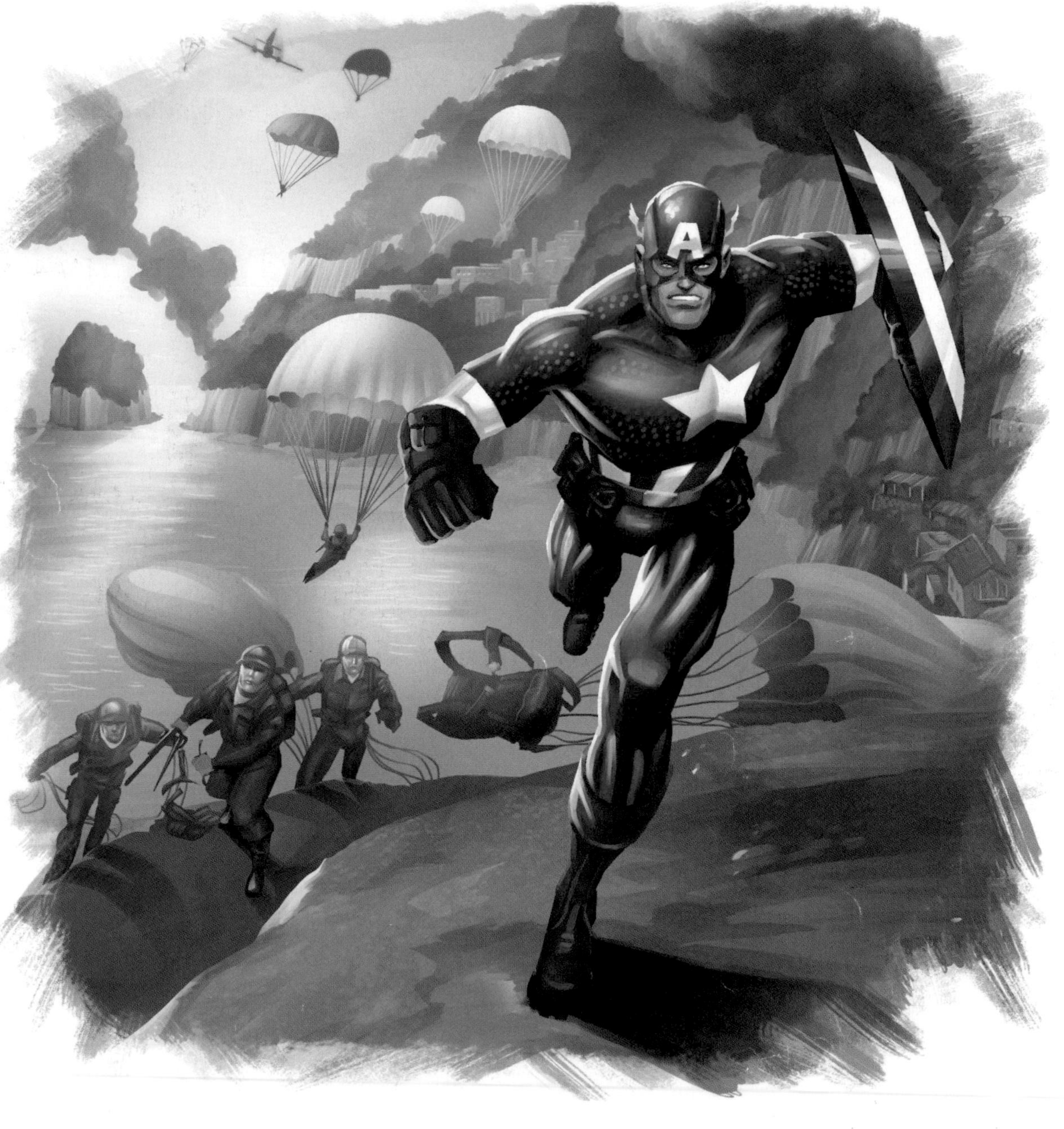

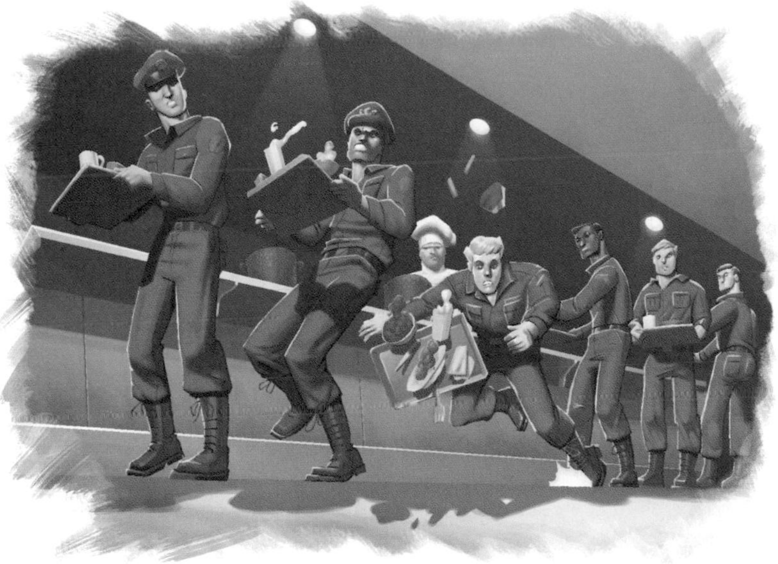

No one ever suspected
that the worst private
in the US Army

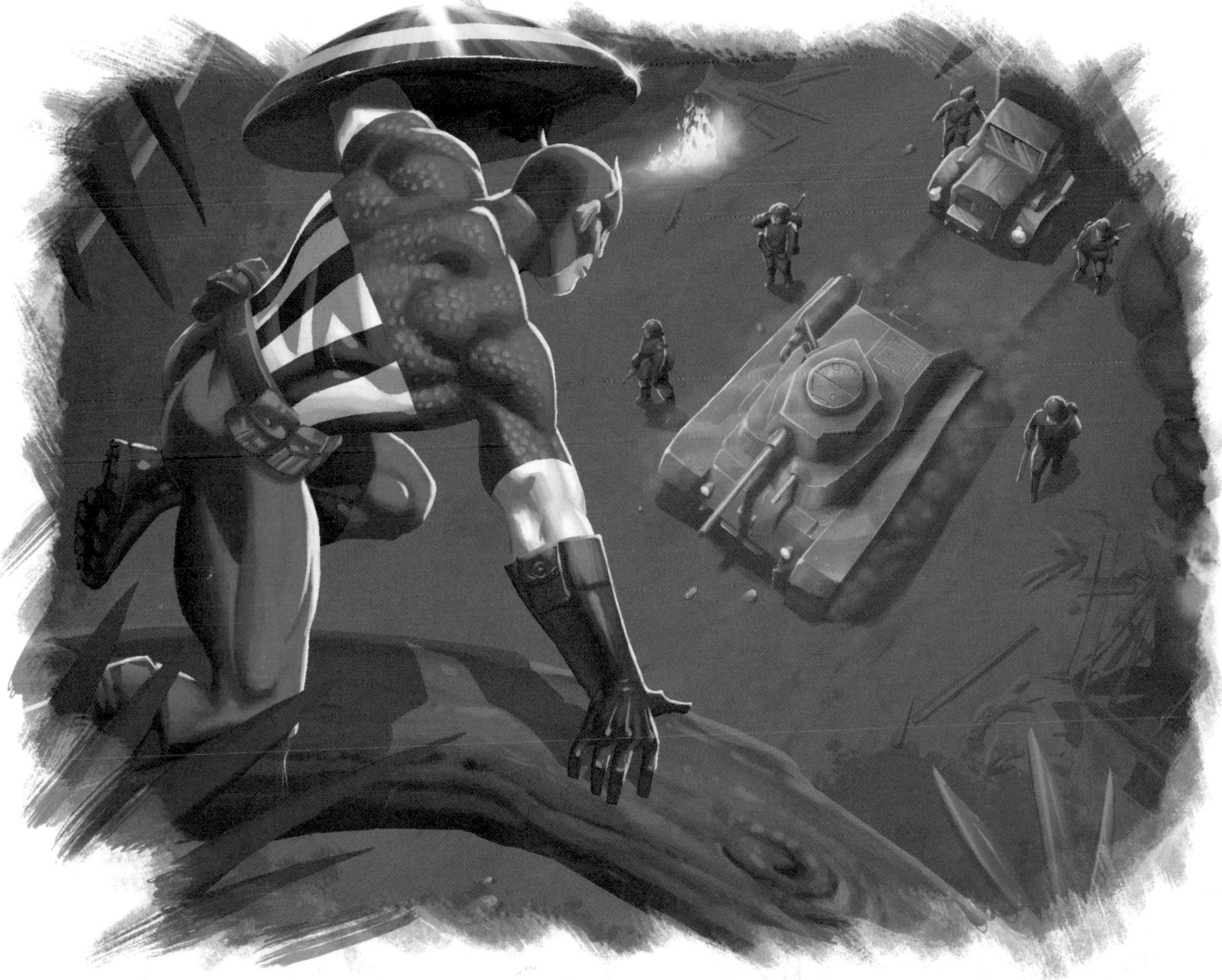

was also the **best soldier** that the army had.

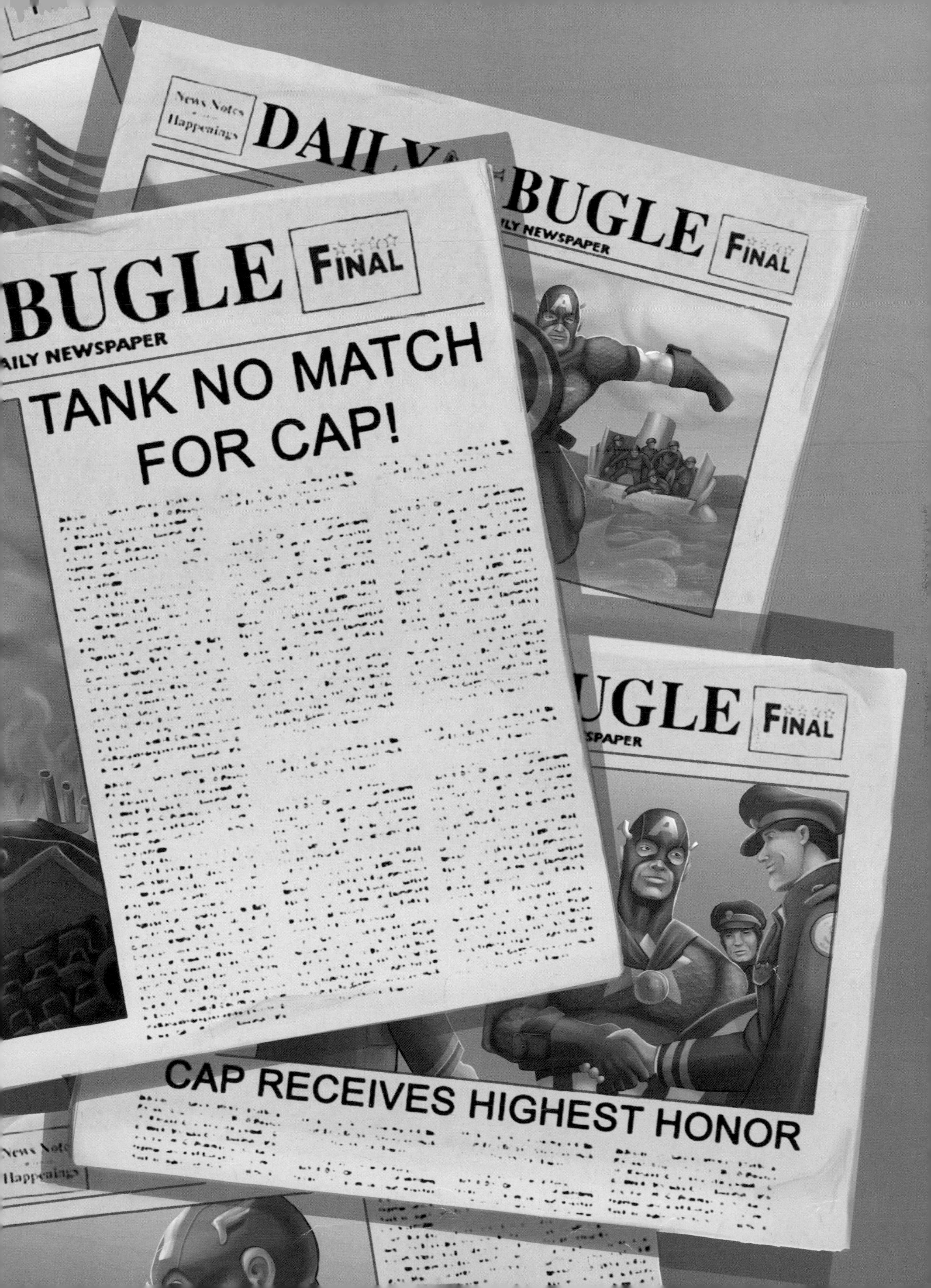

News Notes
Happenings
DAILY
BUGLE
FINAL
BUGLE
FINAL
AILY NEWSPAPER
TANK NO MATCH FOR CAP!
UGLE
FINAL
SPAPER
CAP RECEIVES HIGHEST HONOR

Captain America kept on fighting for **liberty**, until finally…

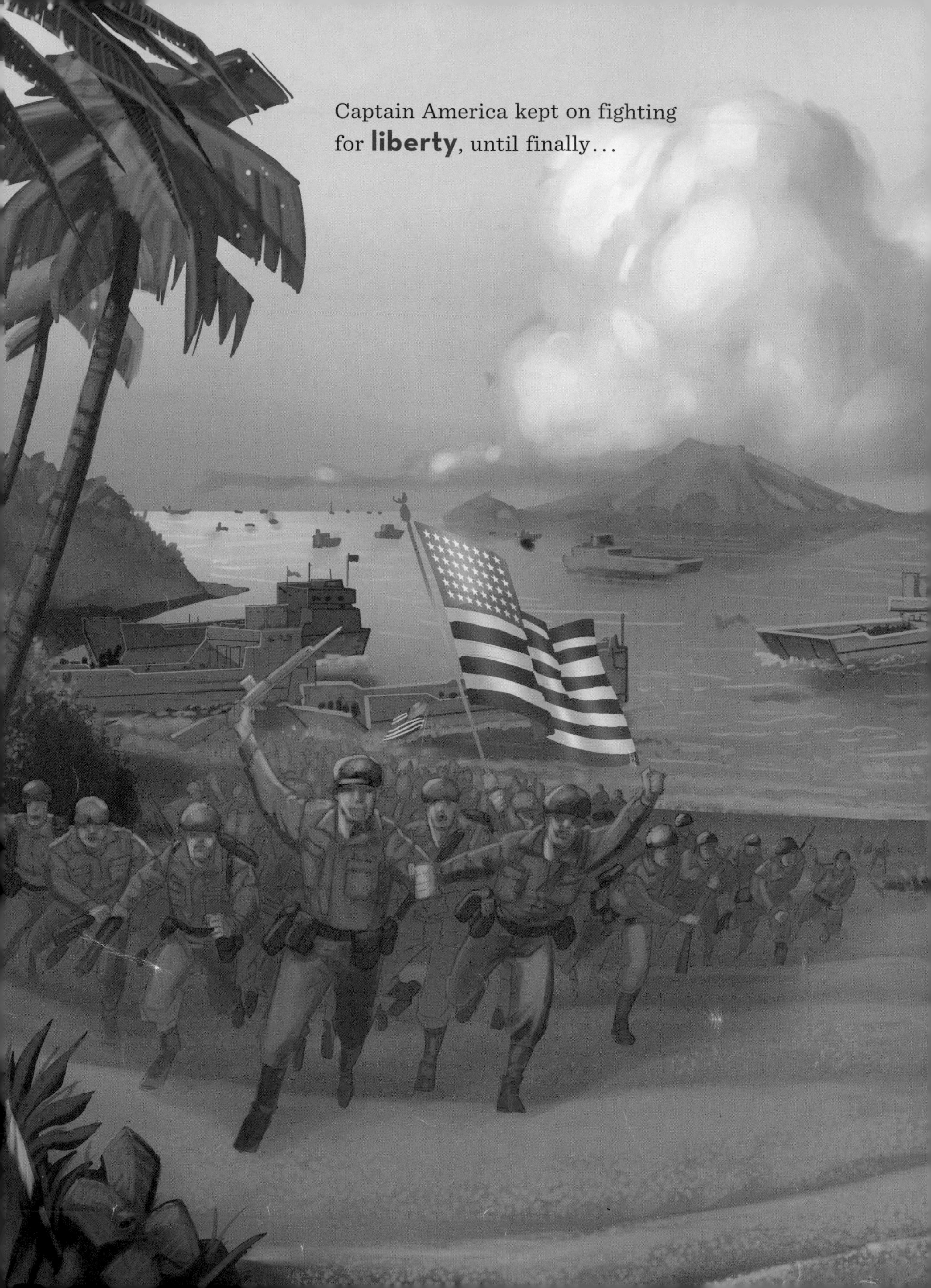

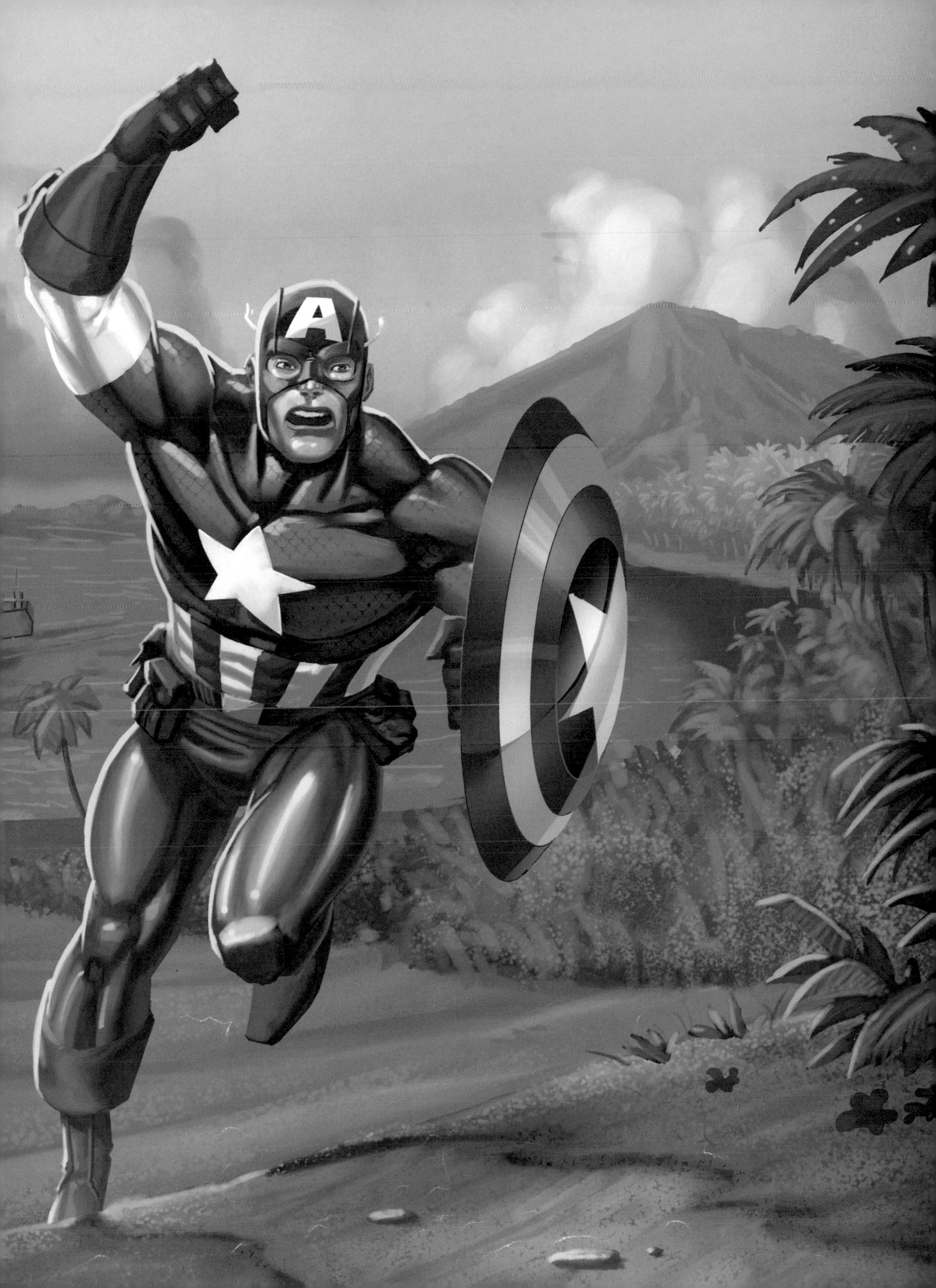

THE WAR HAD BEEN WON.

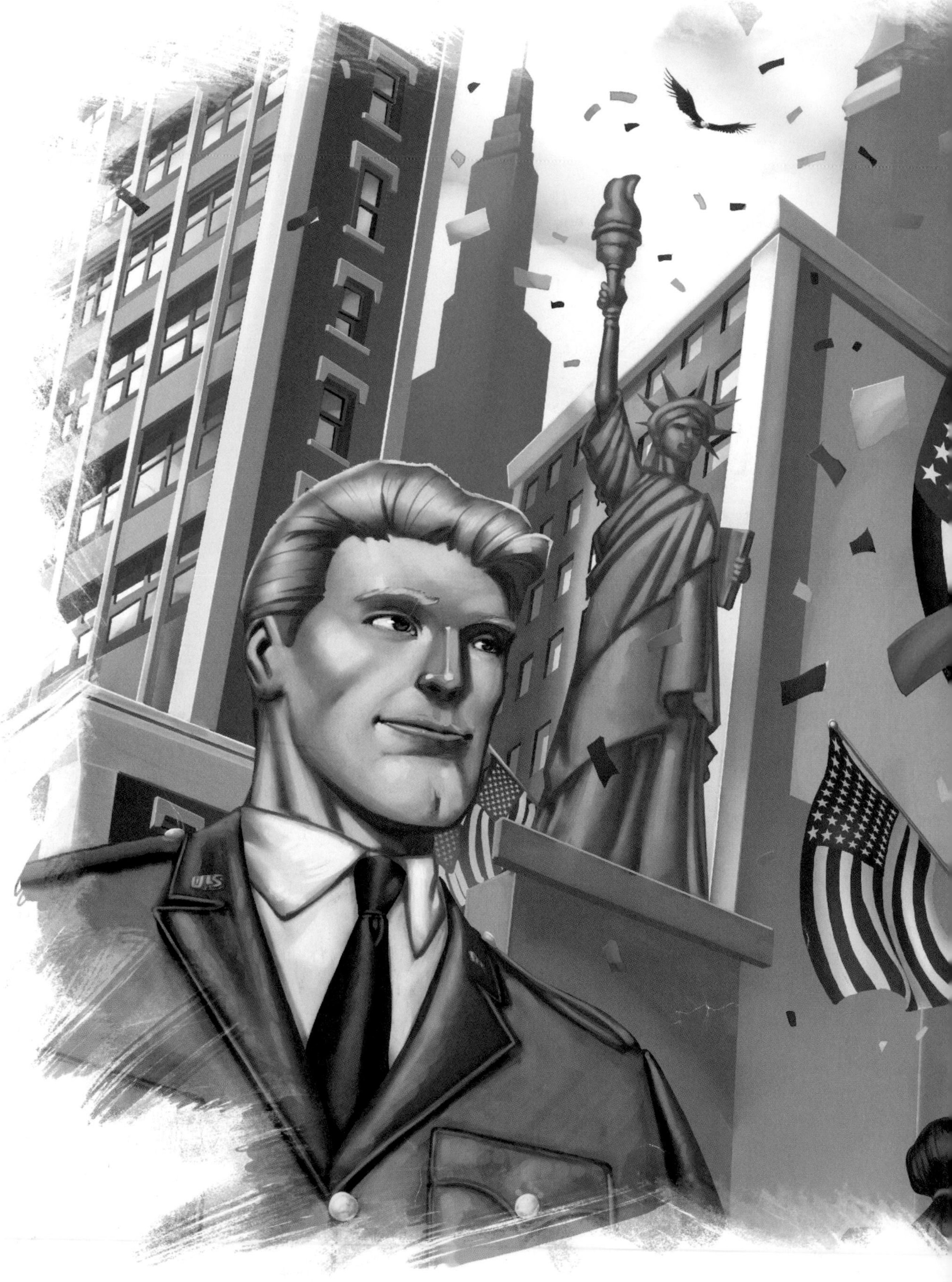

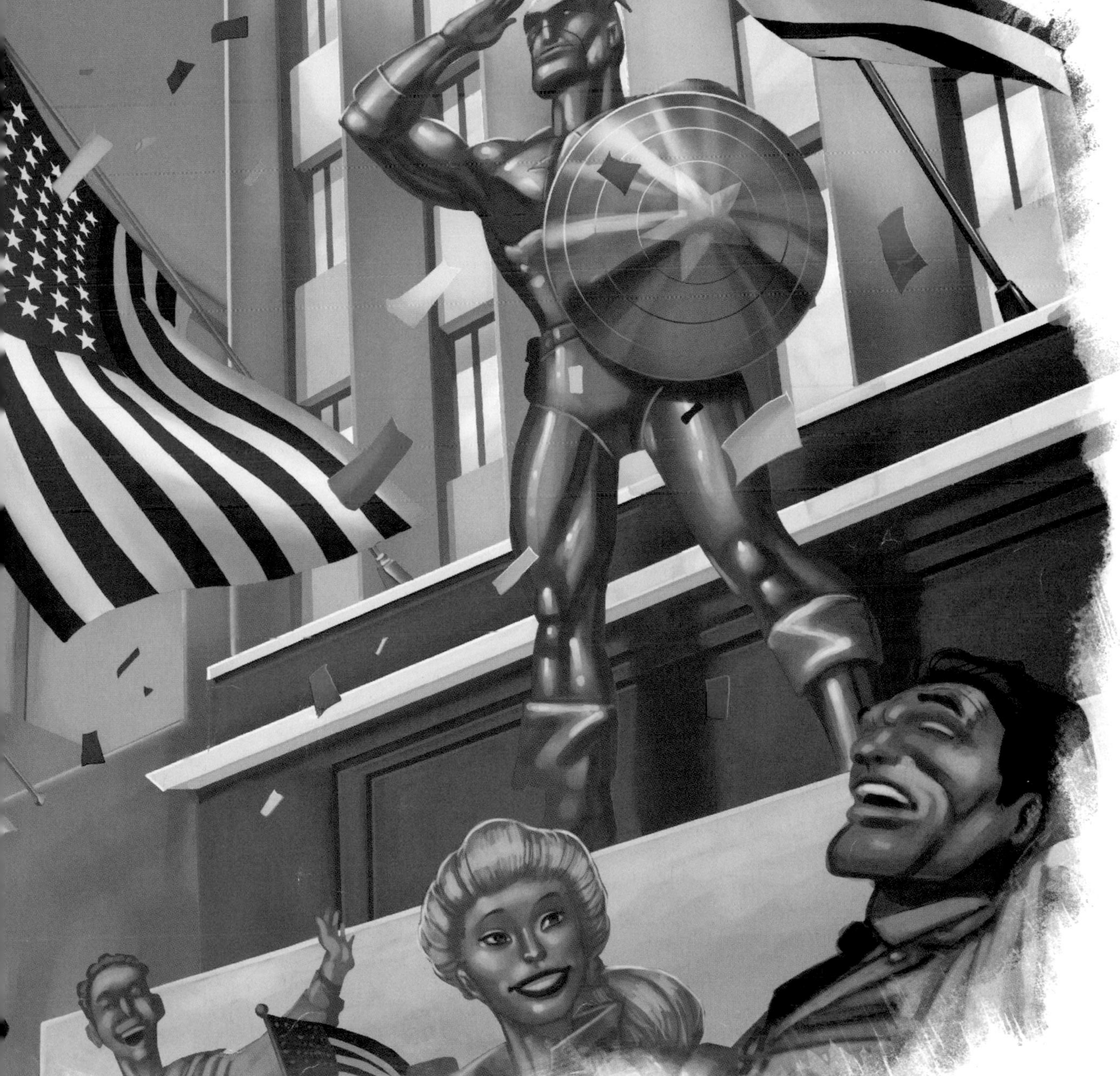

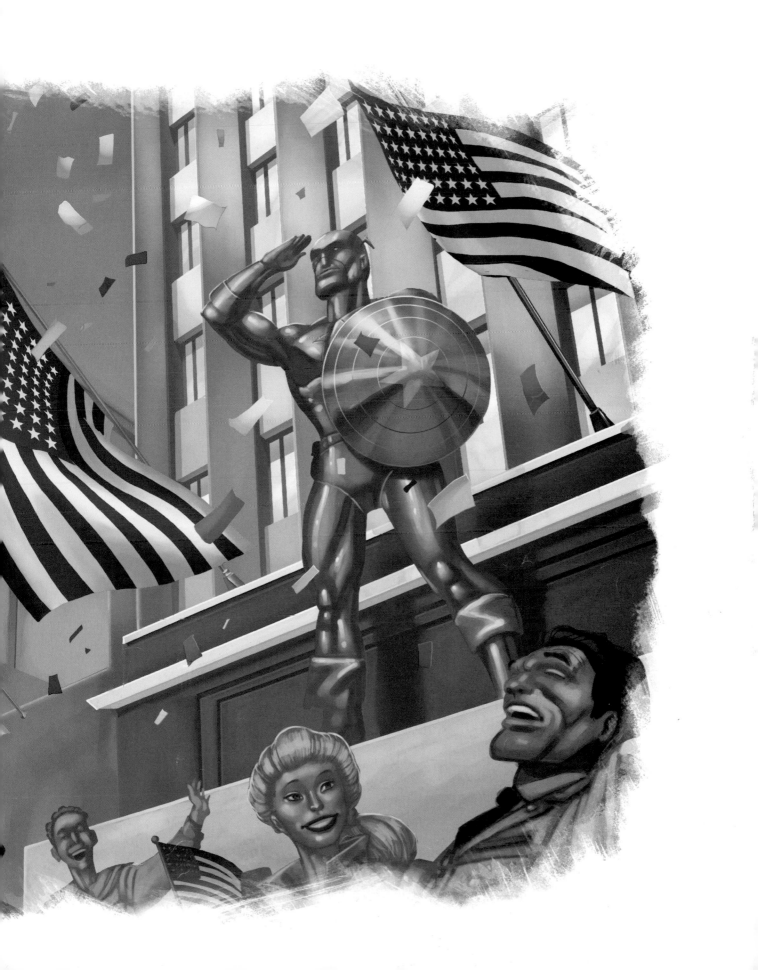

Though the country might not always live up to its promises, as long as Steve was able, he vowed to protect it and its ideals: **justice, equality, freedom...**

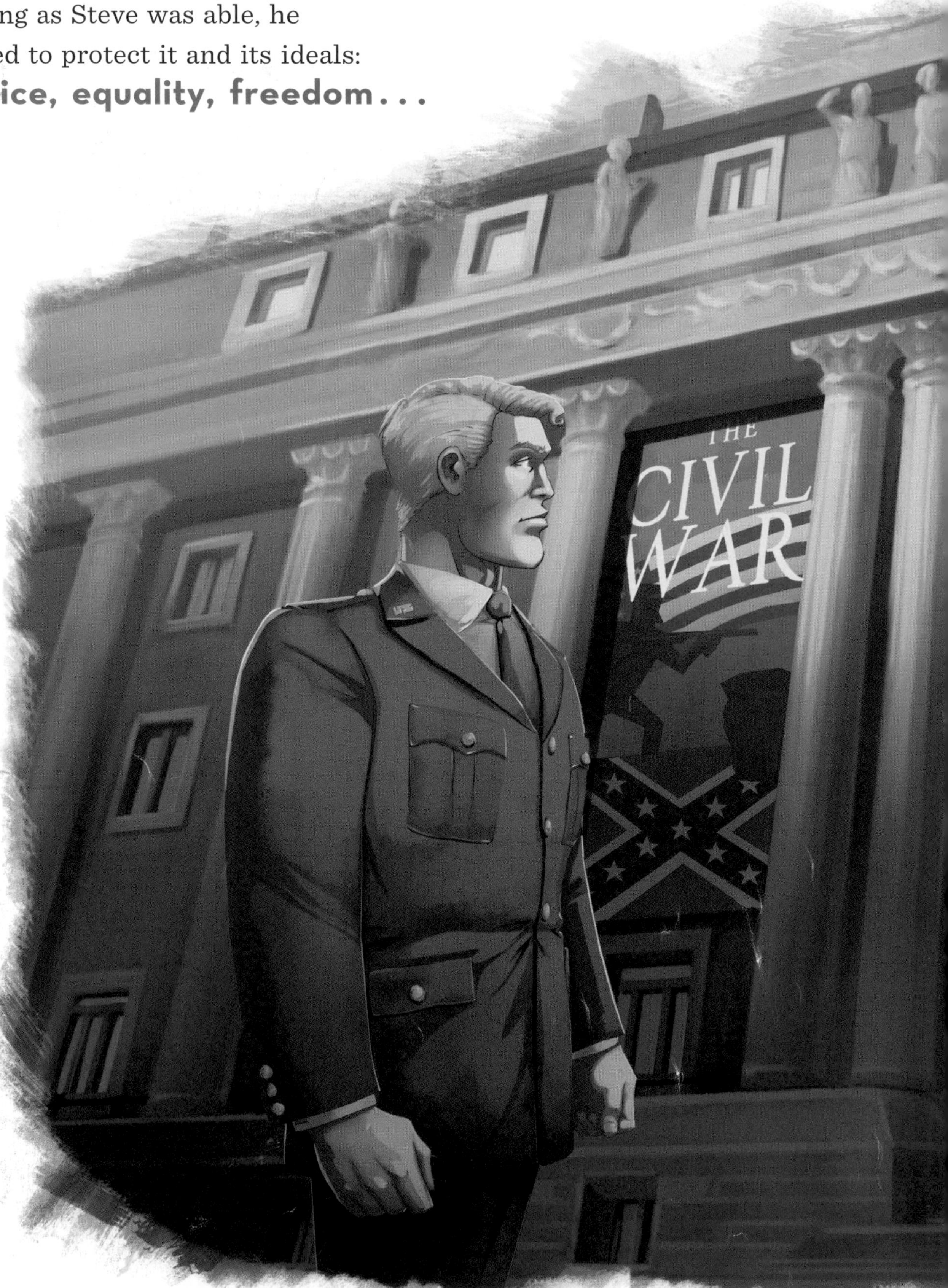
THE
CIVIL
WAR

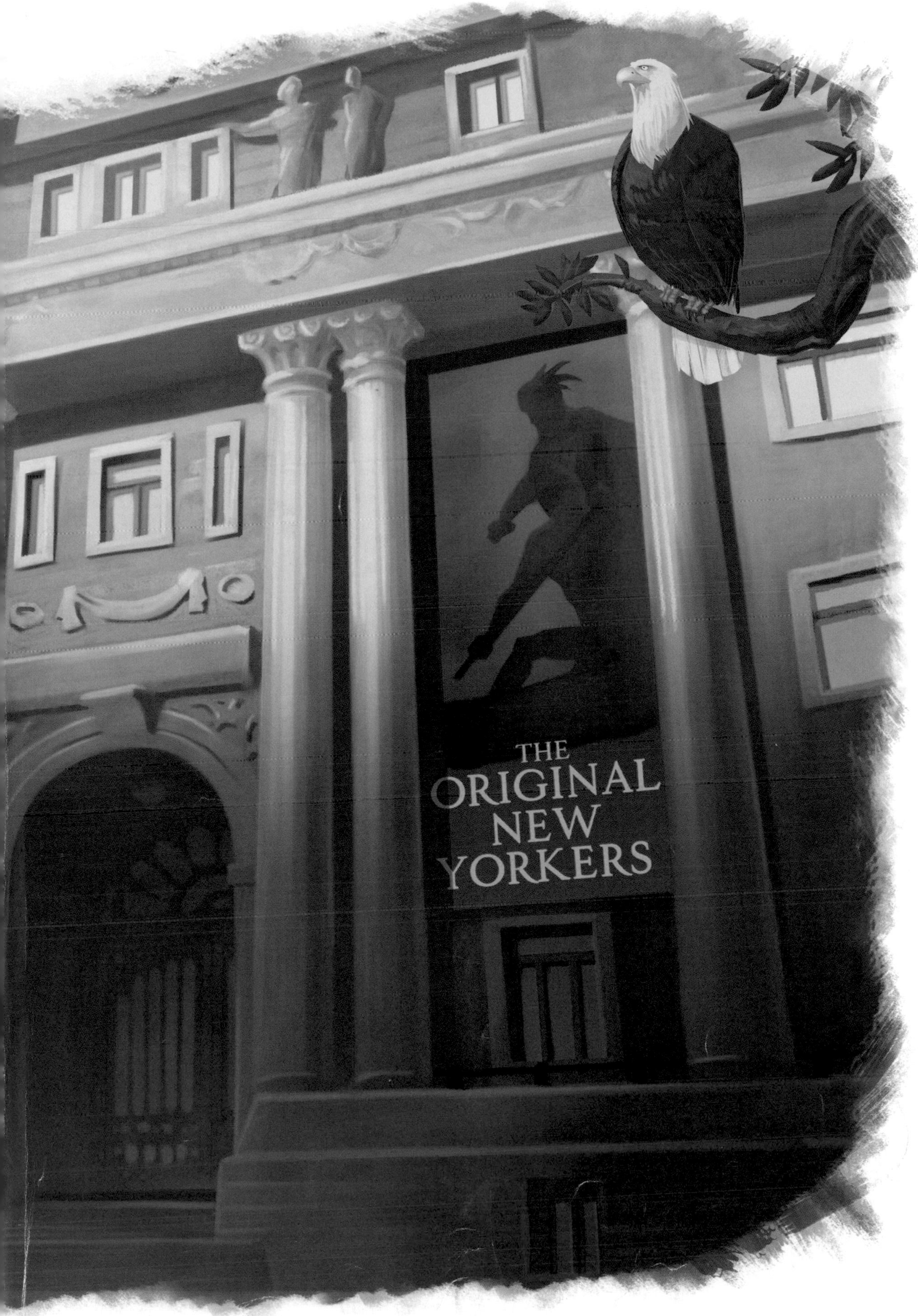
THE
ORIGINAL
NEW
YORKERS

. . . and the dream of what the nation
he loved could accomplish.

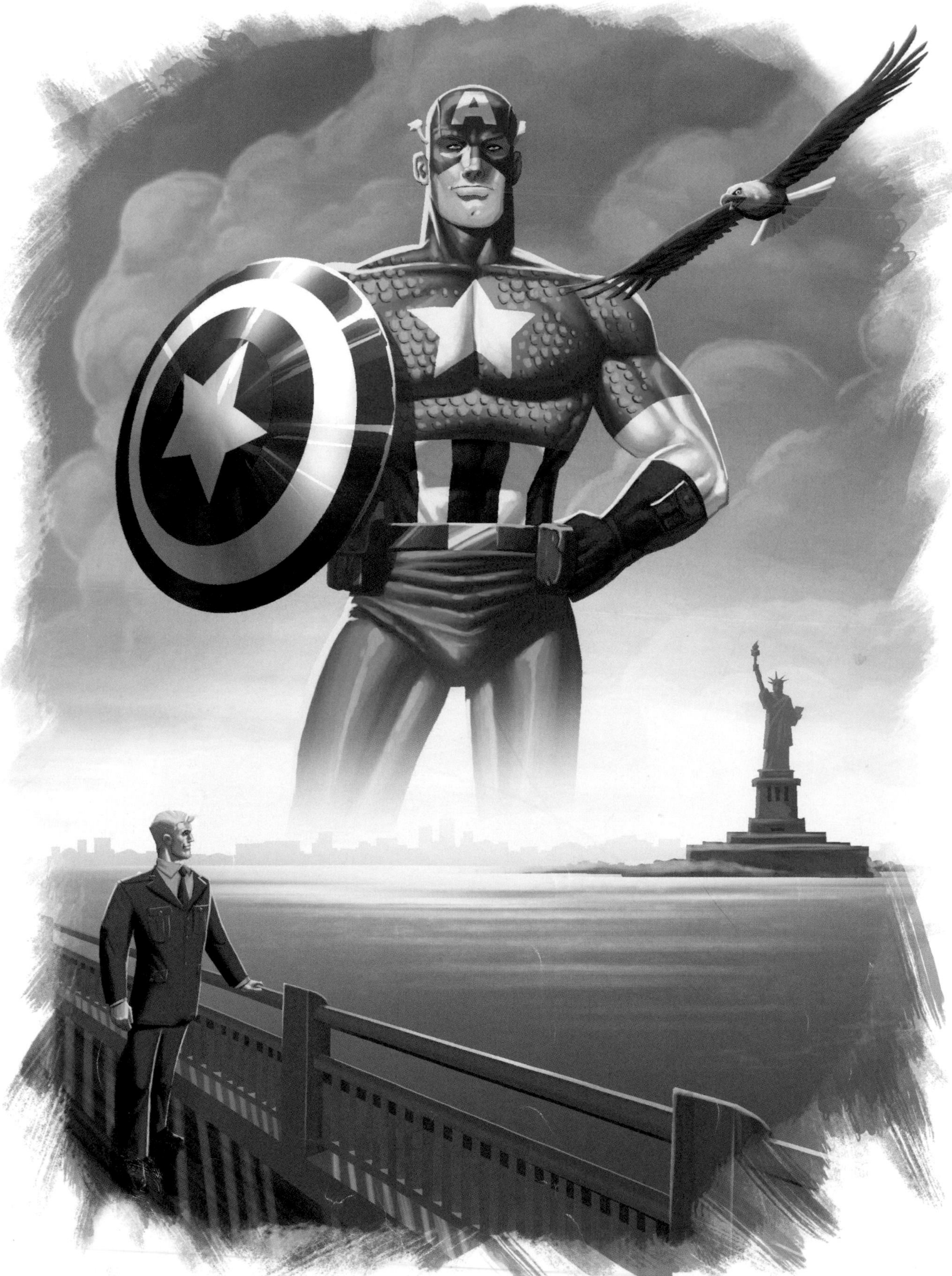